BITTER DRINK

Bitter Drink was first published in 2006 by Roca as *Trago amargo*. Translated from Spanish by Tanya Huntington. Published in English by AmazonCrossing in 2012.

Published by AmazonCrossing
P.O. Box 400818
Las Vegas, NV 89140

ISBN-13: 9781612183909
ISBN-10: 1612183905
Library of Congress Control Number: 2012936529

BITTER

DRINK

F. G. HAGHENBECK

Translation by Tanya Huntington

amazon crossing

To Bill "el Chief" and Silvia,
thanks for the support, the love, and the
real-life inspiration for this novel.
I promise to return the favor.

A man's got to believe in something.
I believe I'll have another drink.
—W. C. FIELDS

Alcohol is the anesthesia by which we endure the operation of life.
—GEORGE BERNARD SHAW

One can drink too much, but one never drinks enough.
—GOTTHOLD EPHRAIM LESSING

I

DRY MARTINI

6 PARTS GIN

1 PART DRY WHITE VERMOUTH

COCKTAIL OLIVES

*C*ombine the gin, vermouth, and ice in a shaker, mix until chilled. Serve in a cocktail glass. Garnish with the olives. Enjoy while listening to Frank Sinatra sing "Witchcraft."

The origin of the best-known cocktail in the world is the subject of some debate. It made its debut in California in 1870. And some contend that it was created by a San Francisco barman named Martinez, while others believe it was first served in the small California town of Martinez. Both theories, however, account for its distinctive name. The drink gained popularity during Prohibition because of the relative ease of distilling gin.

The martini used to be sweeter, with the components mixed in equal parts, than it is today. Though Winston Churchill believed that one glance at a bottle of vermouth was enough, most agree the olive provides the final touch and—according to many mixologists, modern-day alchemists—absorbs the evil spirits in the gin.

American par excellence, the symbol of soirées, style, and class, the martini has been the preferred drink of Hollywood stars, writers, and even presidents for decades—from Humphrey Bogart, Raymond Chandler, Dorothy Parker, and Luis Buñuel to Franklin Delano Roosevelt and John F. Kennedy, to name a few. The last take of the day on a movie set is known as the "martini shot."

Some call it by the elegant nickname "silver bullet." Its simplicity is what makes it so marvelous: only two ingredients are required to create something so sublime.

He wasn't as tall as he looked in photographs, just slightly shorter than a palm tree. His voice wasn't that deep either, only a notch lower than a lawn mower. He puffed on a cigar the size of a rolling pin, perfuming the entire set. His face, underneath the panama hat jammed down over his ears, radiated power—a god looking down upon mere mortals. He embodied the kind of power possessed by those who run the movie business. And that's the only power that counts here.

The director was barking out instructions to his people: actors, producers, technicians, assistants, the locals hired as extras, and dozens of onlookers surrounding the cameras, all working to make his dream, his film, a reality.

I felt sorry for the lot of them, soaked in sweat in this debilitating climate. I, on the other hand, was drinking a martini so dry it drove away the oppressive humidity. And Richard Burton, who was sitting next to me, had just finished his. He ordered another. A double.

I wondered in which leg he stored all that booze. He was carrying around more fuel than the gas plant that powered the set's electricity. Burton spent so much time at that bar you'd have thought they planted him there a hundred years ago. And, as long as they kept the drinks coming, he'd stick around for a hundred more. He was playing an alcoholic reverend in the film, and given how much he had been drinking, I thought he deserved an Oscar for his work off the set as much as on.

A reporter with a face like a cockatoo asked Burton if Elizabeth Taylor was annoyed to find herself in a remote Mexican town surrounded by snakes, tarantulas, mosquitoes, and scorpions.

"She's one tough cookie. But that's Liz. She walks so dainty and looks like a French tart," he replied in his thick Welsh accent, while chewing on an olive, his lunch for the day.

I turned my attention to the scene they were filming: a conversation between "Lolita" and the "God-Fearing Woman." To me, and probably the rest of the world, Sue Lyon would always be Lolita, her most recent role before this one. But she was more renowned for playing the lead in every man's erotic fantasies. Her childish body, crowned by that wicked angel face, simply reeked of illicit sex. One look at her and you could almost taste twenty years of prison. But it was just a front. That chick was more baked than last year's Christmas turkey.

I never liked Deborah Kerr's acting in the first place. But, as the God-Fearing Woman, I liked her even less. She reminded me of someone on my mother's side of the family. We have a saying in Mexico about people from Puebla, something to the effect of not wanting to touch them with a ten-foot pole because they're vermin. And there's a kernel of truth to that.

Ava Gardner was the only star missing at that moment. She was playing a mature woman this time, a former lover of Burton's character, determined to have sex with all the macho men in town. Miss Gardner was back in her bungalow rehearsing for the role. She'd locked herself in with a crooner from a local bar, and it sounded like she'd found her necessary motivation; her cries were so embarrassingly loud that Gabriel Figueroa, the famous Mexican cinematographer, had to turn up the volume on his gramophone. *Carmen* could be heard everywhere, punctuated by the sounds of Miss Gardner's climax and the warbling of the cinematographer's off-tune tenor.

My boss, producer Ray Stark, flashed me a smile, as he surveyed the impressive set built on scenic Mismaloya Beach, as if to welcome me to paradise. But I'd misread his expression. He wasn't welcoming me to heaven; he was welcoming me to hell.

All of the actors on *The Night of the Iguana* hated each other, and there was more sexual tension on the set than at a high-school dance. The director was so sure they would end up killing each other that he'd had five golden pistols made, each loaded with five silver bullets, a different name, including the producer's, engraved on each one. The director was a cautious man; he didn't include any bullets engraved with his own name. Even so, Mr. Stark seemed happy with everybody and everything.

I didn't know why he was so happy with me. We were so different we must have descended from different apes. He'd done everything imaginable in his life, and he was famous and a millionaire to boot. All he had left to do was write a book.

As for me, well, I didn't know what I was yet. For that, I guess, you need an entire lifetime. I'm just a beatnik blood-hound by the name of Sunny Pascal, half-Mexican, half-gringo, half-alcoholic, half-surfer, half-dead, half-alive. Hell, I even speak half *español, mitad* English.

And I was in hell.

Two days earlier they'd found one of those silver bullets in a body so dead not even the flies would land on it. One of the actors had done it. My job was to keep everyone out of jail. Let dead dogs lie.

The roar of a motorboat suddenly shook everyone at the bar out of their inebriated haze for a moment. A glowing Elizabeth Taylor, clad in an eye-catching pink bikini, dis-embarked. If she was the incarnation of sin, as the Catholic Church seemed to believe, then she was the juiciest piece of flesh since Mary Magdalene.

Richard Burton, still clutching his drink, was clearly aroused by the vision.

"See! Now she's even dressed like a French tart!" he told the reporter.

The gossip-rag photographers started firing their cameras at the world's most infamous couple. I finished my martini, enjoying the three-ring circus they'd staged.

The backdrop of the Mismaloya set was truly beautiful from any angle—the mountains, the sea, the deserted beach, all the sunrises and sunsets framed by still-virgin jungle— making the enormous tangle of cables and lights seem even more tawdry. Modernity had certainly overtaken this place, raping it like a vulgar sailor.

The director appeared next to me.

"Keep an eye on them, Sunny. There are more reporters in Puerto Vallarta than iguanas." He threw his cigar into the tiny, listless waves that lapped at the rocks.

I didn't say anything. Hardly anybody said anything to John Huston.

II

THE ZOMBIE

1 PART DARK RUM

1 PART LIGHT RUM

½ JIGGER OF BRANDY

1 PART ORANGE AND PAPAYA JUICE

1 PART PINEAPPLE JUICE

TWIST OF LEMON

1 PINEAPPLE SLICE

1 MARASCHINO CHERRY

1 MINT SPRIG

Mix the rum, brandy, and juice in a shaker or blender with ice. Serve in a tiki glass with a twist of lemon. Garnish with the pineapple, cherry, and fresh mint. Enjoy to the 1963 Ventures's hit "Let There Be Drums."

Perhaps the most famous tiki drink, the zombie, was created in the 1930s by California restaurateur Donn Beach in his famous Hollywood establishment, Don the Beachcomber. Beach used rum, a favorite of alcoholics and sailors, in his cocktails because it was cheap, but by mixing in fruit juice he tamed the rum's strong favor, making it a more universally popular spirit.

The story goes that Beach first concocted the zombie for a regular customer who had a hangover. Returning to the Beachcomber a few days later, the lucky recipient claimed the drink made him feel like the living dead. Donn's blends were esteemed by Clark Gable, Charlie Chaplin, Buster Keaton, Groucho Marx, and Marlon Brando, making him the most famous mixologist in California, and the founding father of tiki culture.

The Cuban Missile Crisis had gripped the nation less than a year ago, but the world had gone back to normal since, and it almost seemed as if nothing had happened.

"I ordered you a zombie, Sunny," Scott Cherries announced.

I'd just walked into the Luau Bar in Beverly Hills, and my drink was already waiting; the cherry welcomed me blushingly. In one corner of the bar, one of those new bands that bred like rabbits in California was trying to convince the small, jaded crowd that they were worthwhile by playing a catchy tune called "Surfin' Bird."

Scott Cherries was drinking from a ceramic tiki glass, the kind featuring a sphinxlike Hawaiian god or the face of a Tijuana cop, depending on your perspective. Scott flirted with the barmaid, a dark-skinned girl dressed like she was from the Pacific Islands, though no doubt hailed from some little Mexican pueblo.

Scott and I were born the same year, but he looked older than me. His mileage gave him away: he's the kind of Republican who has a haircut like Ike's, and nearly as bowling-ball bald, and wears glasses with ruthless frames and a shirt with stripes like a racetrack.

I took a swig from my glass. The first sip was as refreshing as a splash of ice water. I almost asked for a towel to dry myself off. It wasn't even five o'clock yet, but it was already too late in the day for a zombie, surf music, and Scott Cherries. Especially Scott.

Scott was one of those new independent producers that Hollywood was hatching almost as fast as surf bands. Since the recent downfall of the major studio empire, anyone with a camera could make a picture it seemed. Scott's group had truly transformed cinema. Though, sometimes a cheap Roger Corman film was more effective than a couple of Valiums. At least in the drive-in, you could get a little fresh with your girl.

Scott took the movie business very seriously. He knew everything and everyone from Sacramento to Tijuana. He had a knack for public relations, hearty greetings, and cocktails. I stuck with the cocktails.

His angle was book rights: comic books, pulp fiction, even a tome on the life of Duke Kahanamoku, the original, and greatest, surfer. If a director wanted to do a movie on Mighty Mouse, he'd have to go through Scott first. In Movieland that was a flush. Royal, to boot.

Warner had just bought the rights to an old Dr. Seuss story from him. He used the dough to rent an office on Sunset Boulevard and buy a convertible Jaguar. I'd have given my Woody and both kidneys for that car. It's a real dreamboat. They probably sell it with the blonde included.

"Did you bring the photos?" he asked eagerly. "I hope you kept your mouth shut. It's sensitive."

I didn't argue. No one likes to appear in the papers in a photo taken in the men's room of a restaurant in Ensenada. Less, when it's not technically a restaurant, and even less, if the bathroom isn't exactly a bathroom and the men aren't altogether men. If you were Rock Hudson, it would be catastrophic. They'd let Doris Day get away with a tryst with some guy in a restroom but not her beau.

"I had to pay more than we'd agreed. Some judicial cops had the photos."

Hollywood doesn't like to do business with cops, especially not Mexican ones. That's why they call me. If they needed to clean up a mess—like paying a bribe in Tijuana, or going to Rosarito because Sal Mineo flirted with a waiter there—call Sunny Pascal. *He's a beaner, a greaser; he can get his hands dirty.*

I hate them.

As if most gringo producers, stars, and politicians didn't stink worse than a gas-station bathroom.

"Thanks, Sunny. I owe you one," Scott said. He opened the envelope, careful-like, so no one else would see him. He asked the barmaid for an ashtray, and then burned the evidence right there.

Scott always gave me jobs like these. He knew a guy who knew a guy who knew somebody who could take care of sensitive matters. And that somebody was me. Don't get me wrong, I was very grateful. It meant I could pay the rent on a nice little apartment in Venice Beach and send some money back home to Puebla. Mamá always told me she didn't need it, but she never sent it back either.

"I was with a man the other night," he said, changing the subject. Though, there was no need, he knew I'd never ask about the photos. "Ray Stark," he said the name like it was as well-known as President Kennedy's. "He produces Broadway shows. He's married to Fanny Brice's daughter."

"I don't like the theater," I told him, taking another swig of the zombie. "I've got enough of my own family drama."

"He made loads of money as a literary agent. A ton of dough. Worked with Raymond Chandler. He told me some stories."

He gave me that look that only real friends can give, the ones entitled to smack you in the head and call you a jackass.

"Only someone as nuts as you would work as a detective in Hollywood just because you read his stories."

"I don't like the detective bit. I prefer 'personal security.' It's on my business card."

Scott was always laughing at my business cards. Printing the word *detective* on them was too cliché, but working in Hollywood as a detective was a cliché anyway.

Not long after I arrived in California to live with my father, I realized it wasn't such a hot idea. So I struck out on my own. I loved the movies, the surf, and a redhead in Culver City and saw no reason to go back to Mexico. The "personal security" bit had been Scott's idea.

"We ended up talking about you," he remarked.

"Why? You're thinking of selling him the rights to my life story?"

"He's going to start producing movies with outside financing, far from the long arm of the studios," he continued without hearing a word I'd said. "And it's gonna be big. He's hired John Huston to do his first picture. He's got the rights to a play by Tennessee Williams."

"And you're considering me for the main role? That's sweet of you, but my left profile doesn't look so great on screen."

"He's filming in Mexico. In a beach town. Portal Vallarta."

"*Puerto* Vallarta," I corrected him.

The gringos couldn't care less about butchering Spanish. If Cervantes could hear half the things they say to me, he'd turn as pinko as Nikita Khrushchev. Together, they'd have bombed Washington, DC, Manhattan, and Disneyland by now.

"They want someone who can solve problems if anything should happen. You know, deal with local officials."

"Why should there be any problems? It's just a movie."

Scott ordered another round. He didn't answer me; he was wearing that smile that only the cartoonists at Warner Brothers can reproduce. The one Sylvester the Cat sports when he thinks he's caught Tweety.

"Are you in? It's easy money. They're filming at this great spot; you can have a few margaritas, get in some surfing, and shack up with a local girl."

He still hadn't answered my question. Sylvester was written all over his face.

"Good money?" I asked.

"More than what you'd get from me, shoveling the manure of two-bit stars south of the border."

The rum had done its job. Sylvester the Cat was looking pretty good after all.

III

MINT JULEP

2½ OUNCES KENTUCKY BOURBON

4–10 MINT LEAVES

1 TEASPOON SUGAR

1 PART MINERAL WATER

*R*oughly chop the mint leaves to release their flavor, and combine with the bourbon. Add the sugar and mineral water. Serve in a short wide glass.

The venerable mint julep is the drink par excellence of the South and certainly without which no Kentucky Derby would be complete. Historians believe it first made its appearance as long ago as the eighteenth century and describe it as a fortifying drink of the well-to-do colonies in North America: "A refreshing cocktail for the little ladies and gentlemen of society, who enjoy it in the morning when vigor is what they seek."

The mint julep was possibly derived from an Arabian drink called julab, which featured rose petals. The North American variety uses the less pretentious mint leaf. In the beginning, it was prepared with whiskey or any other liquor on hand. But with the rise of the Southern distillery trade, using Kentucky bourbon became standard. The mint julep became as emblematic of Dixie as cotton plantations, Scarlett O'Hara, and General Lee. Enjoy it on a balmy afternoon on the veranda while listening to Elvis's rendition of "Look Away, Dixieland."

———————————

The job interview wasn't held in any of the producers' offices but at a table at the Beverly Hills Hotel restaurant. No secretaries were there to greet me, just a waiter who smiled like a toothpaste model. I'd made an exception regarding my standard-issue guayabera today. Instead, I wore a black suit, a starched white shirt, and a thin tie like the kind Steve McQueen preferred. But I hadn't shaved. I didn't want to look like I wanted the job that bad.

Ray Stark and John Huston were absorbed in a backgammon game when I approached the table. They drank mint juleps, like Southern plantation owners. I stood in front of them with my hands in my pockets, still wearing my dark sunglasses. The Los Angeles sun is harder than acid on the eyes, evidenced by the devastating toll it had taken on the judgment of the city's hottest fashion designers, apparently.

"Sunny Pascal," Ray Stark said.

"You got it right on the first try. Congratulations," I replied.

"The security guy?"

"I see today's your lucky day; that's two in a row. Maybe my business card was a big help."

"Sit down. Just let me finish beating this fuckin' Mick."

John Huston didn't say a word; he just smoked his cigarette. Stark moved a piece. Huston ground the butt into the ashtray and grunted.

"Do you drink?" Stark asked, signaling the waiter.

"Only on days that end in a number," I replied with a smile. "I believe today is one of those…Martini, dry."

The waiter took off like a shot. For service like that, I could only imagine the size of the tips Huston and Stark must leave those lucky devils.

"John is flying to Mexico tomorrow. The set is almost finished. We had a few problems with the bar concept, but the filming *is* going to revolve around it, despite statements to the contrary made by Mrs. Kerr and Miss Lyon."

"Sue's just a kid. She doesn't know anything," Huston spat out.

"They wanted a 'vice-free' set. But who wants that?"

I took a seat next to Stark just as my martini arrived. The olives were so big, they looked like boiled eggs. I thanked the God of alcoholics that they didn't taste like them, though. It was a goddamned amazing martini; the kind they only know how to make in Beverly Hills.

"Scott Cherries told us a lot about you," Stark said.

"Only good things, I hope. The rest is public knowledge."

"We'll be down there for about three months," he continued. "I wanted to film in Acapulco, where the play is set, but

John insisted on Mismaloya. He and his Mexican friend are going to build a hotel down there. After we're gone, they'll be able to rent it to tourists. Isn't that a sweet deal?"

"Better than selling ice cubes to Eskimos."

"This Irishman managed to snag the best possible cast. But I don't think they come in trouble-free gift wrap."

Huston crushed another butt in the ashtray, which suddenly disappeared, a new one materializing in its place courtesy of our attentive waiter.

"We've got Richard Burton, fresh from *Cleopatra*, who'll be traveling with the queen herself, Liz Taylor. They're already living together, even though the ink on her marriage certificate with Eddie Fisher is barely dry."

"Didn't she convert to Judaism for that wedding?"

"Son, here in Hollywood the only religion that matters is the religion of fame. Anything else is just a pretext to skip parties on Sunday or Hanukkah," Huston growled, taking me by surprise. I'd assumed he hadn't been listening to our conversation.

"Michael Wilding will be there too. He's Burton's agent. He came very well recommended by his ex-wife, Liz Taylor. These Brits are really weird," Stark concluded as he threw the dice, rolling a double four. "Ava Gardner is flying in from Madrid; she wants to make a comeback. She seems to have grown bored with bullfighters and Deborah Kerr's ex-husband. She's in the film too, by the way. The girl's role will be played by Sue Lyon, who's about to marry a married man."

I finished my martini, and another magically appeared before me. This waiter was better than Houdini. Stark continued, "John's more excited than a kid at Christmas. He loves the idea of making this movie with all these neurotic people. He even had pistols made for them!"

"Beautiful. Did you get them life insurance, too?" I asked, trying to be funny.

"That's exactly what I meant. If they don't kill each other, I just might."

"And where do I come in?"

"You're supposed to keep that from happening," Stark said simply.

It was all clear as water. Crystal, one might say.

"I assume Scott spoke to you about my fee: it's weekly, plus expenses."

"You're in. When can you get to Puerto Vallarta?"

"As soon as I receive my first check. Am I supposed to keep nosy reporters from snooping around?"

"*Au contraire*, they're free publicity. We want them to find out about everything, but we don't want anybody to end up in the hospital, or worse, a Mexican jail," Stark said, turning back to the backgammon game.

As I tipped the last drops of my second martini into my mouth, it occurred to me that this might be the last peaceful drink I'd have in several months.

IV

MARGARITA

1 PART WHITE TEQUILA

2 PARTS COINTREAU

JUICE FROM 3 LIMES

SALT

1 LIME SLICE

*B*lend the tequila, Cointreau, and lime juice in a shaker with ice until chilled. Serve in a wide glass rimmed with salt. Garnish with a slice of lime. Savor with the song "Tequila" by The Champs.

Despite popular misconception, the margarita isn't an authentically Mexican drink; it was in fact created for or by Americans, depending on which story you believe. Its invention has been attributed to both restaurateur Carlos "Danny" Herrera of Tijuana, who first prepared it for actress Marjorie "Margarita" King, an exclusive tequila drinker; and Margaret Sames, a rich Texan, said to have offered it to guests at her Acapulco home. The invention of this drink significantly boosted the consumption of tequila around the world. Regardless of its origins, the margarita has become synonymous with fun and relaxation on Mexican beaches.

Two days later I began my voyage south to my country. My homeland. My shabby suitcase was pathetic. It didn't even deserve to be called a suitcase: all it contained was two bottles of gin, one of Lolly Pratt, a worn edition of Jack Kerouac's *On the Road*, a week's worth of guayabera shirts, a few changes of underwear, a bathing suit, and my Colt. I decided to drag my surfboards along as well.

I drove from Venice Beach to San Diego, parking my Woody outside the marina so I could see the big aircraft carrier docked there. It was enormous. I couldn't help but whistle, the way you do when you look up at the Empire State Building, or when a wide-hipped, dark-skinned girl walks by in East LA.

My father couldn't see me, but I knew he was there somewhere, either in the carrier or around town. I silently cursed his name and headed back to the car. Our father-son relationship would drive a shrink crazy. No Oedipal complex or anything like that, just a complex system of misunderstandings.

At the border crossing at Tijuana, the US immigration people didn't even ask to see my papers. They thought they were finally rid of me. A Mexican guard did ask me if I was carrying any weapons. I didn't answer, just quietly slid a bill into his hand. My Colt never showed its face in customs; I wouldn't want it to catch cold.

It took all afternoon to drive the dusty highways from the border to Tecate, where I drank two beers at a truck stop. The grimy, obese men milling about the place barely registered my existence. I guess my appearance wasn't worth so much as a second glance.

I drove all night and part of the next day until I reached Hermosillo, keeping myself awake with coffee and shots of tequila. I finally collapsed in a ten-peso-a-night hotel and slept for nearly twenty hours. For five more pesos, I got a big slab of meat for breakfast that I could swear mooed when I cut into it. If I kept this lifestyle up, I wouldn't be able to charge the production company much for expenses.

By the time I got to Mazatlán, my Woody—an old, rebuilt Packard with wooden panels and just the front seat remaining so I could load knapsacks and surfboards in the back—was overheating. The mechanic from the local repair shop gave it the thoughtful consideration of a wine taster and then said he could fix it. I decided to leave it with him, not because I trusted him but because he had a great photo of Natalie Wood in a bikini on the wall. Besides, what other choice did I have?

I would've liked to hit the waves while I waited, but it was September and the weather was bad. Actually, the weather is bad almost year-round in Mazatlán; it's like the Chicago of the Mexican Pacific. Just to pass the time of day, I walked into an old bar near the seawall. The only other customer was an American tourist.

I ordered a margarita, deciding that would work nicely to shake off the dust from the highway and clear the cobwebs in my head. The bartender prepared it with all the grace of a juggler from Barnum & Bailey. After the first delicious sip, I realized why retired gringos prefer Mexico. It wasn't the climate; the secret was this drink for little old ladies. One really does find the best cocktails in the oddest places.

I sat on the stool nursing my drink while the bartender listened to zarzuelas and a selection of songs by Agustín Lara on an old record player. Outside, the bad weather had already started ruining the tourists' vacations, as palm trees bent like umbrellas in a gale.

"Bad day for flying, *soldado*," the forlorn tourist offered in poor Spanish.

He was an elderly man, his thick beard as white as cotton, the tips of it yellowed from too much smoking. He wore threadbare army-issue shorts and a sleeveless shirt with so many stains you could see what he had for lunch last year.

"Yeah, you don't have to be a pilot to figure that out."

"I don't fly either, *soldado*," he said.

"I'm too young to have fought in the big one. And the Mexicans only sent one squadron, the 201st. Today they call them heroes."

"Not in the army? Crap! I've lost my touch," he said, disappointed.

The old man sat down beside me.

He spoke Spanish poorly, mixing it with hard English, like a border whore, and smoked long English cigarettes.

His eyes were as blue as a gynecologist's robe. His skin was cured like old leather—a tone only gringos can acquire after years in the sun.

"Sorry to disappoint you. I only did military service. I don't like wars. They say they're bad for your health."

"Not necessary to be in a war to fight, *soldado*," he said.

"My father is a sailor in San Diego," I offered. "I don't know if that counts."

"*Fantástico!* It's in your blood." He ordered another drink.

The bartender handed him a tall glass filled with ice, pouring a healthy amount of clear liquid straight from a bottle he'd removed from the cabinet, then topping it off with Jamaica flower water. My liver twisted spasmodically.

"Russian vodka, the best. Sold by Patricio. From Cuba, *sabes*," the old man explained.

Patricio smiled, showing me the bottle with a trademark juggler's flourish. It was Stolichnaya: the secret of Cuban-Mexican relations revealed in a Mazatlán cantina, and reason enough for the Mexican Secretariat of the Exterior to exist.

"He just wrecked it with that Jamaica water. But to each his own poison," I replied.

The old man let loose a loud guffaw. With his big white beard, he reminded me of a dime-store Santa mocking some poor kid who'd asked for something expensive for Christmas. Goddamned Santa, *pinche* Santa.

"*Soldado*, you're *gracioso*, but no more so than old Billy Joe."

"That's easy to see, señor."

Two dog tags peeked out of the cleft in his shirt. Like the ones the US Army uses for postage stamps on bodies they ship back home.

"So you really are a soldier. Did you mistake Mazatlán for Saigon? They're easy to tell apart; the whores are better here."

"Nah, I'm retired now. No more crazy shit," Billy Joe said softly.

"Yeah," I said with a grin, "nobody needs that shit. Better to spend your retirement bucks on Mexican beer, no?" Steering the conversation back to safer ground.

"Umm. But you're no tourist. Right, *soldado*?"

"Nah, I'm a babysitter to the stars. I keep them from peeing their pants and getting a bad rap for it."

"Mazatlán *muy lejos* from Hollywood."

"Yeah, but I'm down here to work on a film. It's gonna be more fun than a carnival. I even bought myself some cotton candy," I replied wearily.

"Have a good trip to Vallarta, *soldado*," the old man said, climbing off his barstool and then added, "Bad day for flying."

He lifted the box of vodka Patricio the juggler had prepared for him and disappeared out the door.

I finished my margarita. The conversation had left me uneasy. It was like leaving for a trip and trying to remember if you left the gas on.

V

CUBA LIBRE

2 OUNCES LIGHT RUM

COLA (USUALLY COKE)

2–3 DROPS LIME JUICE

1 LIME SLICE

*S*erve one to two parts rum in a highball glass with plenty of ice. Fill the rest of the glass with cola. Add the drops of lime juice and stir. You can garnish with a slice of lime. One of Compay Segundo's songs wouldn't hurt, either.

This drink was born during the Cuban War of Independence in 1895, when the American soldiers who fought against the Spanish army created it to toast their triumph, crying out "CUBA LIBRE! Long live free Cuba!"

The Cuba libre combines the emblematic beverages of the two nations: Cuban rum and American cola. After Cuba was engulfed by the Communist revolution and then suffered a decades-long US embargo, it became more difficult to assemble the drink. One of the new Cuban government's priorities was to create something *similar, a drink that did not require Coca-Cola, a symbol of capitalist oppression, as one of its main ingredients. Today this drink is enjoyed in its original form in both the United States and Cuba, proving that alcohol can bridge all political differences.*

I arrived in Puerto Vallarta after passing through the historic town of Tepic. The small highway south of Tepic snaked its way across what seemed like the entire Sierra Madre mountain chain. By the time I reached the coast, my Woody was going so slow through the little fishing towns that half-naked kids were able to hawk their fruit, dried shrimp, and macaroons as I drove. From the looks of all of these industrious eight-year-olds, this was no longer the virgin territory peddled by the guidebook I'd bought. Numerous other cars loaded with children were cruising that same provincial highway in search of a beach getaway. The ad hoc roadside commerce was merely a response to the new global economy: if there was something for sale, it was because someone else was buying.

Passing through the town of Bucerias near the Jalisco state line, I caught my first glimpse of beautiful Banderas Bay. One of the largest bays in the world, it's frequented by famous people like Cantinflas, Maria Felix, and the president himself, as well as some who aren't so famous, like humpback whales, dolphins, and the odd tourist.

Puerto Vallarta is located on the bay's inner coastline. Houses spill across the green foothills as if they are trying to reach the peak. But they never do. Only one or two make it even halfway to the top. Vallarta possesses not only natural beauty but the vernacular ambience of a stereotypical Mexican town, the kind foreigners like. The only thing missing is the Indian in a poncho and big sombrero leaning against a cactus.

Of course, there aren't any cacti in Puerto Vallarta. Quite the opposite. The vegetation is so thick and lush you wonder why God didn't share it with the rest of the country. This just might be His favorite place. He gave it beaches, jungles, and beautiful women. I guess even God can be selfish.

The main streets are cobblestone, the rest dirt. The urban layout is so simple a child could have designed it: three long streets run parallel to the beach, and the rest head straight to it. A few church steeples peer timidly out from between the red tile roofs and verdant treetops. Modern buildings of a respectable height stand out like mariachis in a jazz band. A decent airport is located a few miles out of town where visitors arrive in search of sun, sea, and cheap drinks.

The locals hurry to escape the sun's rays, seeking the shade of eaves, but the tourists can be easily identified by their beautiful ocher tones—the women by curves so pronounced they attract the attention of passersby like iron attracts magnets.

If that same selfish God did create Adam and Eve, no doubt they're in a hotel lobby here having a rum and Coke with lime.

There are several convenient hotels, but most of the film workers were lodged in bungalows on the set. Even so, no rooms were available. The place was swarming with US and Mexican journalists who'd congregated with their cameras in bars, hoping to get a cover shot for *Life* magazine. I hadn't imagined the level of euphoria that Liz Taylor's relationship with Richard Burton would cause. Everyone it seemed was completely obsessed with the couple. Since the filming of *Cleopatra* in Rome, everything seemed to revolve around these two, never mind the fact that both were still married. I guess infidelity is headline material these days.

I finally secured a room at the Rio Hotel, though I had to give the manager a huge tip to inspire him to evict a noisy reporter from the *Excelsior*. I wanted to raise my expense quota.

My room had a balcony that looked out onto the street, and when I threw the window open wide, I could see the Cuale River, which divided the city in half.

I turned on the fan and ordered two rum and Cokes with plenty of ice from room service. The heat was so unbearable that even the palm trees were panting. All of them. Every single leaf. But it wasn't the heat that got to you here, it was the humidity.

I thought back to the old gringo from the bar in Mazatlán. Something wasn't quite right, like the uneasy feeling of having a piece of food caught between your teeth. And then it struck me: I'd never said I was coming to Puerto Vallarta. How'd he known where I was headed?

I emptied both glasses, one after another, without breathing.

VI

TEQUILA WITH SANGRITA (JALISCO-STYLE)

TEQUILA

2 CUPS ORANGE JUICE

3 TABLESPOONS TABASCO SAUCE OR
POWDERED CHILI PEPPERS

¼ CUP LIME JUICE

2 CUPS TOMATO JUICE

2 TABLESPOONS MINCED ONION

SALT AND PEPPER

2 TABLESPOONS WORCESTERSHIRE SAUCE

1 LIME SLICE

Mix together all ingredients except for the tequila, season-ing with salt and pepper to taste. Serve in a tall shot glass. Serve the tequila in another shot glass, accompanied by a slice of lime. The music of mariachi Pedro Infante will help it go down smoothly.

Born in the city of Tequila, Jalisco, in the early twentieth century, sangrita, a traditional chaser for shots of tequila, was popular among rich hacienda owners who cultivated the maguey plant from which mezcal is distilled. Invented by Romero's widow, sangrita takes away the strong alcoholic flavor of tequila so you can better appreciate the taste of the spirit.

In time, sangrita became an obligatory accompaniment for tequila, its feminine side, if you will. A sip of tequila is taken, followed by one of sangrita. Few drinks mix together so sublimely inside the mouth.

There was no highway leading to the movie set; the commute was either made by donkey or by sea. All the supplies, equipment, and material had to be transported in *panga* motorboats, which set out from a small dock in Puerto Vallarta on Playa de los Muertos: Dead Man's Beach. Bad name for a beach. Bad name for anything. Especially if you're the dead man.

I caught a *panga* to Mismaloya along with some people who were working on the film. Our little boat skirted the scenic coastline, passing by places no modern man had ever set foot on. Not that I think many modern men are too interested in setting their feet someplace so filled with mosquitoes and vermin.

We reached a spot where two big islands, large and steep, emerged from the sea.

"They call it Los Arcos. That's where all the birds nest," the *panga* captain told me. And indeed, these islands seemed to be a popular spot; an infinite number of birds flew around them: seagulls, pelicans, frigate birds, and other fish thieves. As the *panga* approached the shore, the birds rose up in cacophonous flight.

A few minutes later, the *panga* reached a small beach, pleated like a sheet. Next to it, on a crag, was a colonial-style edifice right out of a Speedy Gonzales cartoon. We'd arrived at *The Night of the Iguana*.

We disembarked on a dock built at the foot of the rocks, and then climbed a steep staircase that had been built between the outcroppings in an attempt to make this lost corner of the world more habitable. A great flurry of activity greeted me once I reached the plateau. Dozens of people moved back and forth, like a colony of ants, carrying, dragging, or delivering things. Just a typical day on a film set.

I bumped into a man wearing a sky-blue guayabera and creased linen pants that were so smooth they walked on their own. He sported several days of stubble and several years of receding hairline. I guessed he was one of the production assistants, as he clutched a thick stack of papers to his chest like it was his virginity.

"I'm looking for Mr. Stark," I ventured.

"If you hurry, you can catch a plane to Los Angeles, darling. He won't be here until next week," he answered me in Spanish tinged with a touch of Pasadena playboy.

"Mr. Huston?" I tried again.

"Sure you want to see him? He hasn't filmed anything since yesterday. He just might swallow you whole."

"If I can't have the big boys, I'll settle for you. I'm the security guy. Mr. Stark told me to show up here."

Sky-Blue Shirt smiled. He turned around, signaling back to me. He didn't shake my hand or introduce himself. He was no gentleman. But then, no one in Movieland was.

"Follow me," he replied. "They've been expecting you since last week. Did you make a wrong turn in Tijuana?"

I followed my new acquaintance, who swayed his hips so much it looked like he was dancing a rumba. His style was unmistakable—of the Rock Hudson/Sal Mineo variety.

"You got a name? Or should I use 'Hey, you!' like everyone else?" I asked.

"Gorman, honey. But if you want to play rough, you can call me some other name."

I smiled. I liked it when pretty boys flirted with me. "Sunny Pascal. Are you the production assistant?"

"Costumes, makeup, scenery, or the guy who brings Miss Lyon her cookies and milk. Today I'm busy handing out scripts. Want one?"

"Not a bad idea, although I already know how the story ends," I said, taking the script Gorman offered. "Is it any good?"

"Nothing you couldn't buy for a song on Sunset Boulevard. Maybe a couple of Oscar nominations. Not best picture or best screenplay," Gorman replied. He was obviously quite the film critic.

When we reached the bar on the set, the stars and production crew were taking a break, escaping the blazing heat.

Gorman introduced me to the production assistant, the director's assistant, and another assistant of some kind. They didn't even turn to look at me. I was no more than a contractual obligation to them, a burden imposed on them by Mr. Stark. Nothing more.

The last assistant I met told Gorman he should see to it I had everything I needed. Looks like Mr. Gorman just got promoted from milk-and-cookies boy to my new production liaison. I don't know if he saw it as a promotion or not; he merely winked at me.

"And what's your job here supposed to be, bloodhound?" Gorman asked.

"I thought you might be able to tell me that," I replied, taking a seat at the bar so I could take in the scenery.

"Seems to me you just won the lottery," Gorman said, taking a seat next to me. "Nothing's going to happen here. Maybe some yelling or a catfight. Just some material for *The Hollywood Reporter*."

The barman was busy preparing some virgin drinks to be distributed among the extras. I wondered how far my influence as "the security guy" would stretch.

"You want something to drink, Gorman?"

"Tequila sunrise, darling," he purred, then turned to the barman, and snapped, "Don't be stingy with the cherries."

"A martini," I told the barman, then added, "I'm in charge of security."

The barman hesitated, but then turned and started working on the order. In the movies you don't bet on someone's looks, you bet on their name tag—a clear chain of command stretching back to Lumière.

"If you let me in on what's going on around here, I'll buy you another round," I offered Gorman.

He produced a pack of cigarettes from his pocket with all the masculinity of Katharine Hepburn and lit one up. He took one long pull, and half of it turned to ash before my eyes.

"The movie has got to be finished in less than three months. I don't foresee any difficulties. No special effects, not many extras. It's a filmed theatrical play, darling. We just have to pray the weather will be merciful. But the weather has no mercy at all; she can be a real bitch."

"How many are there?"

"Members of staff? One hundred and twenty people. Almost all of them are housed in the bungalows. They built us bathrooms, living rooms, dining rooms…It's like a hotel."

"What about local workers?" I asked.

"Tarascan Indians. They live in a village on the beach, fishing and catching iguanas. Now they're the construction crew."

"Mexican modernity."

"Thanks for the drink," he said, standing up. "I've got to finish delivering scripts."

"If you see or hear anything, I'll be around."

"Count on me, but be careful, macho man, aluminum bends both ways."

I caught sight of a swift boat that had just reached the dock of the set. Several elegant people disembarked, all wearing dark glasses and expensive clothes. Two faces were of particular interest, the others, their assistants, were recyclable.

Liz Taylor wore a cotton robe that stuck to her perspiring body, and Richard Burton had completely unbuttoned his shirt against the oppressive heat. Behind them a retinue followed like a royal procession. They were accompanied by, among others, their agents Hugh French and Michael Wilding, Taylor's first husband, now reduced to picking up after the horses in the parade.

A man just a hair smaller than a concession stand stopped at the foot of the stairs, his hands at his waist. He wore a guayabera that could have doubled as an awning, and sported a red bandana knotted at his neck and a pair of yellow snakeskin boots, as flashy as two neon signs. His straw hat was bigger than an umbrella, and his face was as wrinkled and cured as barbecued meat. If not for the mustache, you could eat it in a taco.

This was unmistakably the famous Emilio Fernández, better known as "El Indio." Movie director, actor, typical Indian-Mexican character. Typical like pyramids, typical like tequila.

He gave a shout, opening his enormous arms wide to embrace Elizabeth Taylor. After he released the poor thing, you could have swept her up in a dustpan and thrown her into the nearest wastebasket.

"Come with me, Liz! All of you: follow El Indio. You'll be all right if you stick with El Indio," he announced.

Emilio Fernández took out a .45 bigger than a Nazi how-itzer and aimed it at Richard Burton's chest. Even from my perch I could tell that Burton cursed under his breath, no doubt in Welsh, and foamed at the mouth like a rabid dog.

The sight of the gun sent a wave of adrenaline through me. A wave I couldn't surf, one that broke right in my face. And I jumped down from the bar stool and barreled toward the group, my Colt drawn.

Fernández, pistol in hand, continued pawing Taylor as if she were a piece of fruit at the market, as my right fist found El Indio's jaw.

He dropped the actress, though my blow didn't seem to affect him any more than that. He didn't budge, not one inch. That was typical too, like the pyramids.

My Colt looked like a toy gun against the mass of this man. His two eyebrows joined in the middle to form a fero-cious, King Kong expression. I didn't relish the idea of being perforated by a .45. Those cannons cause wounds that don't even hurt—because you're too dead to feel them.

There was no shot, just a fist the size of a medieval bat-tering ram right between my eyes.

Then a slow fade to black. I'd won myself an intermission.

VII

HURRICANE

1 PART DARK RUM

1 PART LIGHT RUM

1 PART ORANGE JUICE

1 PART MARACUYÁ JUICE

1 PART PINEAPPLE JUICE

1 PART SWEETENER

1 PART GRENADINE

DASH OF LIME JUICE

1 ORANGE SLICE

1 MARASCHINO CHERRY

Mix all the ingredients in a cocktail shaker or blender. Serve in a high hurricane glass shaped like a lamp. Garnish with the cherry and orange slice.

The hurricane was invented during World War II in Pat O'Brien's Bar in New Orleans. A creative barman decided to serve the cocktail in a hurricane lamp from a big candelabra, the kind typically found in those parts, thus giving the drink its evocative name. The bar is still open today, boasting the one and only original recipe for this drink emblematic of the Big Easy. Enjoy on a warm night to the sounds of "When the Saints Go Marching In."

————————

The lights came back on in my head. And as I opened my eyes, the glow was so intense I couldn't stand it.

"Turn off the spotlight," I cried.

"Sorry, the sun has a contract to be here for another six hours," a female voice replied, brightly. She had the kind of voice that comes wrapped in a nice package. A diva's voice, I concluded.

"So give him a big tip and maybe he'll go away."

I focused front and center. Not bad, not bad at all. She was blonde, the kind of blonde that'd make all the other blondes feel inadequate. Big green eyes, a dreamy expression. Lips like a ripe peach. Anything you asked for, whatever you wanted, she had it.

The beautiful face holding an unlit Camel between its lips came into focus. "Welcome to the world of the living. Can I get you anything?" she asked.

"Two tequilas. One for my mouth, the other for my cheek."

I was lying down on an *equipal*, as life on the set went on around me. Nobody cared that I'd checked out for a while. Everyone was continuing business as usual, except for the beautiful blonde and a smiling Gorman who was covering his mouth with a pink handkerchief.

"What happened to Miss Taylor?" I asked.

"She's having a drink with Mr. Fernández," Gorman answered, pointing toward the bar.

Around a table, the Indian bellowed with laughter alongside Richard Burton, Liz Taylor, and John Huston.

There I was stretched out on a sofa, my cheek so hot you could fry an egg on it. Some security guy I'd turned out to be.

"You kept him from squeezing her like a tube of toothpaste. You're a hero," Gorman exclaimed.

"What the fuck is El Indio Fernández doing here, anyway?" I grunted, touching my cheek. It felt as big as Texas.

"He's the associate producer."

"It would have been safer to form an association with Hitler. He wouldn't have packed a cannon instead of a pistol," I said, sitting up. The ground spun in circles, like when you get tossed by a wave, or a Tijuana cop demonstrates his boxing technique on your face.

"You're a tough nut to crack," the blonde said as she lit her Camel with a Zippo that screeched louder than a mattress in a cheap motel. "Maybe you ought to think about changing jobs. Yours is a pretty dangerous one. Taming lions or skydiving would be better."

"Someone has to do it, and some days I get to meet beautiful women. I met my quota today." Even playing the tough guy hurt.

"I can see you're feeling better. The smart-ass in you is back already." She exhaled a puff of smoke into my face.

It tasted oddly wonderful, carrying a hint of her perfume.

"Maybe a massage would set me right."

"Don't push it," she said, rising to her feet and sending me an air kiss. "If I'm ever in trouble, I already know which dog will come to my aid."

"Watch out for that dog; he bites."

"I'll be careful, bloodhound," she said sweetly as she walked away. Her white cotton dress showed off the silhouette of her shapely legs underneath like a bar lamp. A bar lamp from a real fancy joint.

Fernández glanced at me. He was still laughing when he got to his feet. He put on his enormous umbrella hat, the shadow it cast darkening his skin even more, and crossed the sun-drenched patio to where I lay.

"You're a Pascal, *pendejo*?" he exclaimed, spraying saliva. "Yep. Your father's that sonofabitch *cabrón* Captain Pascal?"

"He's a commander now, sir," I replied, cringing at the weakness in my voice, but all the toughness had drained out of me as soon as that fist crossed my face.

"Well, if you're that bastard's son, come, *bébete un tequila* with me."

He grabbed my shoulder and lifted me up like a wooden ventriloquist's dummy. Oh, to be made out of wood right now would be a blessing, I thought. My shoulder ached. Everything ached.

"Your father is a real asshole. I met him in Santa Barbara when I was working for the gringos."

"Nice to meet you," I replied, unable to come up with anything intelligent to say to him.

With another affectionate slap on the back that almost cost me a lung, he asked, "Did he tell you why I was dabbling in the movies?" He didn't wait for me to answer. "That *hijo de puta* assassin Huerta exiled me.

"How 'bout that, Pascal? That asshole motherfucker thought El Indio was a troublemaker. So I threw my hat in with the gringos. Fucking around with cinema. That's where I met that *cabrón* father of yours. We'd go to the fairgrounds and pick up *muchachas*. He used to knock up Mexican girls who worked picking oranges."

"We don't talk much," I offered. "But I guess you know he was stationed in the Pacific."

"That bastard only got more tail: Japanese. I bet you've got a yellow sister, *mijo*," he cried, releasing his bellowing laugh.

Everyone around us echoed him. No one followed the joke, but they got the gist. They didn't want to end up like me, ground beef. I've always prided myself on setting a good example.

"Send him my regards, *muchacho*. You all right?"

"I'm just fine. It only hurts when I breathe."

"Wise guy, *chistoso*," he said, and pulled me over to the bar.

"Don't drag me, sir. I think I can manage on my own. I think I can even go to the bathroom without spraying."

"Real funny, just like your old man."

Two shot glasses of tequila were already waiting for us at the bar. He lifted one up to my mouth, the other to his own.

"If I'd known you were a Pascal, I would have punched you again, to knock *lo pendejo* out of you."

He tipped the glass back in his mouth and started roaring with laughter again. His chorus of ass-kissers followed suit.

"So that bastard Stark hired you to take care of us? What a joke, *pinche chiste.*"

I tipped my glass back, the liquid gold sliding down my throat. "I'm sure you'll find it amusing, too, when I ask you to hand over that pistol."

The laugh track disappeared like magic. In the blink of an eye, we were alone and absolute silence fell. Even the birds stopped singing. They'd probably shat themselves in fear.

El Indio Fernández didn't move a muscle, not a single inch of his body stirred. Nothing. He was as cold as a statue of Benito Juárez in a municipal park.

"You can't take it away from me, *hijo.* It's my virility. *Mis huevos.* It would be like cutting off Samson's hair, like cutting off my balls," he said slowly.

"Let's make a deal then," I replied, taking advantage of the liquid courage I'd just ingested. "I have to do my job. I don't like it. It's a bitch having to babysit these gringos. You know they can't drink more than two tequilas without making a scene. But out of friendship to my father, you could give me a hand. I need to make them believe that no one is going to get hurt out here. Keep the revolver and just give me the bullets. I'll take care of them so they don't catch cold or anything. If they start crying, I'll give them back to you."

Given the disastrous outcome of the fight, I had opted for diplomacy instead. Sometimes it worked. Not always. If you don't believe me, ask Kennedy.

I closed my eyes and waited for the next blow. I suspected that it might hurt less this time. Not because of the impact, but because I already knew what to expect.

Nothing happened.

"Only because you're Pascal's son, *cabrón.*" He downed another shot of tequila and unloaded his gun. He slammed the bullets down on the bar. Then El Indio Fernández shrugged his shoulders, gave me a pat on the back that knocked the air out of me, and went back to his guests.

I was reaching for the bullets when John Huston appeared next to me.

"Emilio's only weakness is shooting people he doesn't like. For instance, his last producer," he grunted. "You're lucky he didn't shoot you. That means he likes you. I'm sure he'll settle his dispute with you some other way."

Not the most reassuring words. Huston returned to his actors, and I was alone for a while. I could see in the jungle, beyond the thatched roof where my princess charming had awakened me, a group of Indians watching me with the same expression they'd no doubt had when they used to watch the Spaniards. You could see the question in their eyes: "What the fuck are you doing here?"

They had been relegated to manual labor on the set, these former owners, dispossessed of their lands to benefit the million-dollar movie industry and this film that might win a couple of Oscars. But not best picture, like Gorman said.

VIII

GIMLET

---

3 PARTS GIN

1 PART ROSE'S LIME JUICE

1 LIME SLICE

*C*hill the gin and lime juice with ice, and serve in a cocktail glass; garnish with a slice of lime while listening to Wayne Newton's rendition of "Call Me Irresponsible."

Surgeon and Admiral Sir Thomas Desmond Gimlette (1857–1943) first served the drink that bears his name during the First World War. The Royal Navy officer had access to gin, and it occurred to him to mix it with lime juice.

An icon of Prohibition-era speakeasies, the gimlet is simple and elegant like its cousin the martini, but it has a more feminine flavor. Gimlette was the inventor, but it was Raymond Chandler's character Terry Lennox, in the novel The Long Goodbye, *who made it a legend, declaring, "A real gimlet is half gin and half Rose's lime juice and nothing else."*

I'd never read or seen the play the movie was based on. But it was nothing like the stories I preferred. It centered on an alcoholic reverend, Burton's character, as a sexually obsessed loser and bum. Not so different from the actor himself, actually.

The good reverend, on a trip with a group of old women to a beach in Mexico, sexually harasses the granddaughter of one of his traveling companions, our infamous Lolita. In order to avoid the trouble coming his way, he hijacks the school bus they're traveling in, finally taking refuge in the hotel of a former lover. Residing there are a sketch artist, Deborah Kerr's character, and her father, the self-appointed oldest living poet. All of these characters suffer and yell a lot. That's basically the story. Pretty standard Tennessee Williams from what I can tell.

I couldn't see what an old famous guy like the poet was doing on a beach in the middle of nowhere. If I were him, I'd buy a Jaguar, like the one Scott Cherries owned, and hire a couple of amicable girls. That way I'd die with a dumb grin on my face.

But that's me, not the movie plot, which I found dull. Lots of dialogue and no car chases. When I finally met Tennessee Williams, it all made sense. You can't expect much from a writer who dressed in pale pink and was accompanied by a lapdog wearing red ribbons.

My work on the set pretty much consisted of doing nothing. The bartender kept the drinks coming, and I obligingly tossed them down. Every day of the week was the same. Regular people think a movie set must be so glamorous and exciting, but anyone lucky enough to actually have the experience usually becomes very frustrated once they discover how tedious the whole thing really is. Three months of boring, repetitive, hard reality in order to produce two hours of frivolous fantasy. Giving birth is less painful and more fun for those involved.

Blondie appeared once in a while on the set, trailing behind her friend and charge, Lolita. Gorman revealed that my princess charming was Eva Martinei, Sue Lyon's teacher. The actress was still hitting the books when she wasn't fooling around with her boyfriend, listening to music, or playing at acting. Blondie also ran interference for her pupil. So her mother wouldn't find out that Hampton Fancher, the boyfriend, hadn't only sampled sex with her daughter in the kitchen but on the motorboat, in the sound room, in the editing room, in the car, in the school bus they were using for the shoot, on the beach, in the jungle, behind the bar, and, every now and then, in an actual bed.

Blondie passed by one afternoon as I was downing my fifth drink. She shouted a greeting, flashing that roguish smile. I growled my reply like a rabid dog. But by then I was so drunk, it sounded more like an anesthetized dog about to get spayed.

Nevertheless, she came over and we chatted awhile, volleying picaresque puns. She was a well-read woman of the world, knew everything, had lived a lot, and traveled even more. She was the type of college girl who didn't mess around with lowlifes like me. Sometimes she would disappear for days at a time, and I would try to forget her blonde hair with the help of three extra martinis.

The weather was hot and humid. Whenever tempers ran high among the stars, that same selfish God would send rain our way to cool things off. I imagined He didn't want those puny Hollywood actors spoiling His paradise.

When the rains came, the filming was put on hold and the entire cast returned to the "big city" of Vallarta. There, Huston and Stark wallowed in card games and Ava Gardner wallowed in someone's bed. Richard Burton wallowed in his bottle, and Liz Taylor wallowed in strawberry shortcake. The rest of us spread out to various cantinas.

One of those first nights the rain had driven us back to Vallarta, I put on my best rags—a black, long-sleeved guayabera, clean and stain-free, a pair of black cotton pants, and shiny new huaraches I bought from an old man in the market for less than three pesos—intending to visit one of the cantinas.

I walked down the seawall. A lighthouse illuminated the water that was covered in a layer of fog so dense it resembled an opium den. Several local couples were out strolling. Gorgeous girls tittered and shot me coquettish glances as we occasionally crossed paths. I could hear some tone-deaf American journalists singing Sinatra from a nearby cantina.

On the corner where Morelos Street intersects the seawall, where the old Spanish Customs building was located, a noisy cantina caught my attention. If I were a smoker, I would have tossed my cigarette into the street and entered the joint with all the aplomb of a leading man. But I'm not. So I lifted a piece of pineapple taffy up to my mouth in my best Bogart style and pushed through the door.

The jukebox was playing one of the latest hits by Elvis. On the heels of the King was our own pop-chart singer Angélica María, less blonde than Doris Day but just as virginal.

I pushed past tables chock-full of news seekers from around the world, stagehands from the San Fernando Valley, and curious locals. I felt like I was in some bar during World War II, where beautiful Frenchwomen were only too glad to show their appreciation to US soldiers. For them, and for beautiful Vallarta women as well, it was a one-way ticket out of a constrictive family.

I ordered a gimlet from the bar, but I knew the cocktail wasn't going to be any good coming from a bartender dressed in a kitchen apron. This was a drink that required a professional touch; an amateur could turn it into a major disaster. Still, I wasn't feeling too picky tonight, so when the drink arrived, I finished it in one swallow.

"How is the circus going, *soldado*?" I heard a voice say.

To my surprise, the old gringo from Mazatlán was sitting beside me. I don't know what startled me more: the fact of his being there or that he was still wearing the same dirty T-shirt from before. Only now it bore fresh stains.

"Hey, mister! You really do know where all the fun is," I managed.

"Billy Joe *viva* in town. You are *el forastero*."

"What? You only go to Mazatlán to pick up your Russian vodka?"

"I got other business there," he replied cryptically.

He raised his ruby-colored glass. A Jamaica flower floated between the ice cubes.

We toasted, the glasses clinking like a servant's bell, both of us glad to see a friendly face. For some reason, I liked the old man, despite the fact I found him unnerving. Unnerving but agreeable. Like a little lamb with two heads.

"So you live here?" I said. "Nice place to forget about the war. If you miss wars, come with me one day to the Mismaloya movie set. You'll see some Britons who are trying to rip the guts out of some Americans. Better than D-Day."

"I can see you're not really happy, *no feliz*. What, you can't lead your own mission? That's a VIP place for generals." Cantina philosophy, cheaper than a shrink and always accompanied by ice cubes.

"Hey, how did you know I was coming to Vallarta, anyway? I never told you."

"Kennedy once told me you didn't need to see Khrushchev to know there were Russians in Cuba."

Kennedy? Khrushchev? Cuba? Good questions for an old stranger. "This isn't a good day for you to be pulling my leg. If you want a good laugh, look for another drunk. This one's already too beat up."

He didn't answer me, just smiled and asked the bartender to bring his friend another one of those "girlie" drinks.

Two more drinks appeared on the bar. I was looking forward to a peaceful chat with my new drinking buddy, but someone had other plans.

Before my second sip, I heard a small voice behind me, shrill, as if it belonged to someone who'd taken a bullet in the nuts.

"You must go someplace. It's *urgente, señor.*"

A boy in a dirty school uniform was holding his arms tightly against his torso, like a Christmas nutcracker.

"Excuse me? *Perdón*?" I replied.

"The señorita needs your help. She gave me the address."

The kid handed over a folded slip of paper. "Eva. Miramar 87," it read in hurried, sloppy handwriting. I smiled at the thought of Blondie. Tonight was going to be more than interesting I'd expected.

When I raised my eyes, the kid had his hand out. One day he just might become the best bellhop in the world, once he was old enough to carry suitcases. I gave him a few coins.

"I've got to go to work, mister. Next time, I'll buy the drinks," I told the old man.

Billy Joe smiled, showing me all his teeth like a corncob, but he didn't say anything. I asked the barman for directions to the address on the note and took one more look around the joint. With a little luck, by night's end, some local girl would be arranging her marriage to a gringo technician, I mused before heading out to the street.

IX

BLOODY MARY

2 OUNCES VODKA

3 OUNCES TOMATO JUICE

½ OUNCE LIME JUICE

3 DROPS WORCESTERSHIRE SAUCE

2 DROPS TABASCO SAUCE

SALT AND PEPPER

1 CELERY STALK

Mix the ingredients in a blender to chill. Serve in a tall glass with ice, preferably with salt on the rim. As a final touch, add a stalk of celery to the beat of George Gershwin's "Rhapsody in Blue."

The barman, Fernand Petiot of Harry's New York Bar in Paris, claims to have created an early version of this popular drink, and renowned hangover cure, in the 1920s that consisted of equal parts tomato juice and vodka. When Petiot moved to New York and started working at the St. Regis Hotel, he added some spices to please the more adventurous New York palate.

The origin of the name is not clear, though it has been linked to several women, some real, others fictional: the most famous being Mary I, Queen of England. The drink's nomenclature is likely more modern. Some say it was inspired by Mary Pickford, and others attribute its origin to a patron of Petiot's who upon tasting the concoction confessed that it brought to mind a similar drink from his local haunt, the Chicago Bucket of Blood Club, and a beautiful girl named Mary who worked there.

There was an attempt to change the name to "the red snapper," but it was too late: the legend was already in place.

———————

Four blocks later I reached a long stairway that zigzagged toward the mountain. Puerto Vallarta is like a Minotaur's labyrinth, I realized, cursing the founders of the city for putting this damnable place on a rock to start with. I mounted the stairs, leaving my kidney, one lung, and part of my hernia behind. There was another street at the top of the hill, illuminated by the lamps that shone from every window of the large houses with high walls, like Turkish prisons, that lined the street for as far as I could see.

A few cats meowed as I passed by, and a block or so further, I spotted a new Ford parked in front of one of the larger houses. So there is a way to get up here without suffering a heart attack, I thought. The car was parked in front of a house with the same address as on the note. I touched the hood; it was warm like a schoolgirl's breast.

A rusty bell hung from the old wooden doorway, but the door was ajar and the notes from a jazzy number slipped out into the night. It was from *Birdy*, one of my favorite records. I decided to enter the house without ringing. Bells are only good for calling people to mass or to independence.

In a plant-choked patio like a neglected cemetery, an ashlar angel tried to free itself from a bougainvillea and a few rustic pieces of furniture were scattered in no particular order. I walked as lightly as a ballet dancer toward the music, which seemed to be coming from the room right off the patio, a light tapping accompanying the rhythm.

I crept through the open door and was assaulted by a strong odor that made my nose wrinkle. The scene before me had all the signs of a recent big bash: small tequila glasses, empty bottles, marijuana joints, and a brazier were all strewn on the tile floor. But I could tell right away this was one party I was glad I missed. The distinct smell of fresh blood and a bloodstain on one of the sofas confirmed it. I instinctively drew my Colt.

I spied another open door on the far end of the room. It led to a nearly bare room decorated like a convent. The bed was unmade, and in one corner, wrapped in sheets, a figure, crowned by an unforgettable head of blonde hair, was moving.

She was lying there in the fetal position, sobbing. The stench of vomit made me take a step back. I reached for Blondie's wrist and took her pulse. It was through the roof and her pupils were so dilated, I would have had to use a magnifying glass to find the irises.

Blondie was all right, just a little beat up, and absolutely stoned. Of course, the odor that had welcomed me when I first arrived was opium. The pipe had been tossed aside, next to a broken syringe. Her veins were no doubt a traffic jam of opium, heroin, and marijuana—perfect conditions for a car crash.

"Hey, doggie! I've been expecting you..." she said rasping, her voice like sandpaper.

"Party's over, Blondie. I'm taking you to a doctor."

"Is he gone?"

"Who?"

It was then I realized that the noise I'd heard accompanying the music wasn't part of the recording. It was someone breathing heavily, together with the unmistakable squeal of mattress springs. Blondie hadn't been alone.

Squeezing the Colt, I turned around and started toward the patio.

"Don't leave me!" Blondie cried as I left the room.

As I entered the music room, gunfire greeted me. The good news was that the man trying to put on his underwear was more concerned with getting dressed than aiming straight.

My Colt reacted instinctively. I hit the deck and was still rolling as I snapped off a couple of rounds. The man winced, and I was sure that one of my return greetings had at least nicked him. It hadn't stopped him, though. He closed in fast and kicked the gun from my hand. I took the next kick in the jaw as I tried to stand up.

I didn't see little birds or stars, but it stunned me momentarily—just long enough for the man to get his underwear on and take off running.

By the time I got up, I heard the roar of a motor spreading its wings. The bird had flown the coop.

The room was as sparsely furnished as the bedroom had been, with two exceptions: a portable record player sat in the corner, playing a worn-out 45 over and over again, and next to it a camera was set on top of a tripod. The camera was open, and there was a used roll of film inside. I took it out and slipped it into my pocket.

The bed's white sheets were splattered with blood from the wound I'd given to Mr. Antsy Underpants, and a naked girl was sniffling like a crushed cricket on top of them. She couldn't have been a day over fifteen.

X

HANKY-PANKY

1½ OUNCES GIN

1½ OUNCES SWEET VERMOUTH

2 DROPS FERNET BRANCA

1 MARASCHINO CHERRY

Mix the gin, sweet vermouth, and Fernet Branca in a glass with ice; chill. Serve in a martini glass with a cherry while listening to an operetta by Gilbert and Sullivan.

The hanky-panky was Ada Coleman's idea. Her benefactor, Rupert D'Oyly Carte, was the proprietor of the Savoy Hotel and produced Gilbert and Sullivan operas in London. She gained widespread acclaim for the hotel bar by serving Mark Twain, the Prince of Wales, Prince Wilhelm of Sweden, and actor Charles Hawtrey, the latter of whom once asked for something with a little punch in it. Coleman served him the soon-to-be legendary concoction, and Hawtrey drank it down in one swallow, pronouncing, "By Jove! That is the real hanky-panky!"

No one wants to deal with cops. They're cold, perverse men with bad intentions. In Mexico, you can't even give them that much credit. For a simple misdemeanor, they'll kill you, rob you, and lock you up, in that order.

Some might argue that there are exceptions and that sometimes, in a small town like Puerto Vallarta, they're on the up-and-up and can't be bought. But since my ticket to hell is already reserved, I've got no reason to lie. The cops here are just like all the rest: total sons of bitches.

In Puerto Vallarta, there was no judicial police force. Every now and then a few would drop by from Guadalajara or San Sebastian, but not today. Here there were only local cops, in vulgar blue uniforms and white shirts.

They showed up when I contacted the Red Cross Emergency Hospital via my bellhop messenger boy, who had appeared outside the house. Telephones were still rare household items in this town.

An old ambulance arrived half an hour later, bouncing along the cobblestones. Blondie was just an overdose, although her face had been through a remodel. Nothing that couldn't be fixed, though, with plenty of rest and a raw steak.

As for the other girl, she turned out to be my bellhop's sister. He of the fidgety underwear had picked her up on the seawall under the pretext of taking her to a party, a private party, as it turned out, that consisted of giving her drugs, getting her drunk on tequila, and then deflowering her.

There wasn't much to be cured there either, except for the sorrow of her mother, who wept as if her child were dead.

But they weren't going to let me off the hook that easy.

The cops were rubbing their hands together at the thought of the political hay they were going to make. This house hosted a drug distribution network and had become a refuge for perverts. The scoop would sell like hotcakes to the mob of journalists searching for juicy prey.

Sergeant Quintero, short and brown as a mushroom, was one of the top dogs on the force. His face wore the scowl of a sad old mutt. He wouldn't take his hands out of his pockets, not even to say hello, and he walked with his eyes on the ground, as if life had already beaten him down. Sergeant Quintero explained everything so halfheartedly a mannequin could have done better.

The sergeant posed for the journalist's photos with his bored mastiff expression, and when they had taken their fill of pictures of the place, they moved the party to some bar down near the beach.

It had been decided that the names of the victims would not be divulged, and when Sergeant Quintero and I were alone, he told me, "We don't like people sticking their noses in, especially outsiders." His tone was so nonthreatening I almost laughed.

"I'm with the gringos, but I was born in Puebla."

"I don't give a shit. *Mis huevos!*" he answered, shrugging his shoulders.

"The man who shot me wasn't American," I said. "I couldn't see his face, but I'm sure whatever he wanted to cover up with his underpants wasn't stuck to some white guy."

"We don't like smart-asses, either," the sergeant reminded me.

"I'm only here so the people working on the film don't get into trouble. I'm sorry about the little girl, but that's your business. As for sticking my nose in, you can take it, keep it, and water it every week," I said, walking toward the door.

"You already knew your girlfriend was a lowlife, *verdad*?"

"No. But if you want to fill me in on the local gossip, just pass the soap and let's do some dirty laundry," I answered, turning around.

"That blonde lady has been telling everyone she knows all about drugs. That she's spent up to three weeks smoking opium. That she's traveled the world in search of new experiences. *Una especialista*: a real gourmet on the subject."

"People can do whatever they want with their lives. I left mine behind in a bottle of tequila."

"The young lady has already been booked. Her boss, the child actress, is the one who's made sure she doesn't end up in Guadalajara with the *judiciales*."

"Don't tell me that just because Sue Lyon talked pretty you sat up and listened?"

"A donation always helps, compadre."

I looked down on that little bugger Quintero. I felt even more like squashing him when he smiled up at me.

XI

TOM COLLINS

2 OUNCES GIN

1 OUNCE LEMON JUICE

1 TEASPOON REFINED SUGAR

3 OUNCES CLUB SODA

1 MARASCHINO CHERRY

1 ORANGE SLICE

Combine the gin, lemon juice, and sugar in a shaker half filled with ice cubes. Strain into a tall glass of ice and add the club soda. Garnish with the cherry and orange slice to the smoky sounds of Julie London.

Some say the name comes from Old Tom, a brand of gin from the turn of the twentieth century that was much sweeter than today's offerings. Others claim the drink was named after its inventor, an Irish immigrant who worked as a bartender in New Jersey. Collins apparently concocted it for his friends to enjoy after a long, hot day of work, something refreshing to raise their spirits. The drink became so famous that even the long, tall glass it's traditionally served in is known as a Collins glass.

———————

Less than a week later, *Siempre!* published a detailed feature article entitled "Infamous House of Vice," focusing on the depraved lushes filming *The Night of the Iguana*. Something had unleashed the wrath of that rag. Perhaps our mere existence was enough to provoke vitriol. In Mexico you can be despised for less. "Our innocent children, ten to fifteen years old, are being introduced to sex, drinking, drugs, vices, and carnal bestiality by this group of Americans: gangsters, nymphomaniacs, alcoholics, and heroin-addicted blondes…" the article stated. The magazine even beseeched the government to expel John Huston and his group. "It's not too late. Responsible, patriotic Mexicans can still save the beauty of Puerto Vallarta," *Siempre!* intoned.

"A long time ago, I stopped caring about attacks in the press. Besides, I'm too busy shooting a film to waste time on 'carnal bestiality,'" Huston amusingly replied to an American journalist regarding the accusations. And with that pronouncement the interview was over. The entire crew laughed and applauded. I did the same from my security post at the bar. We had to live up to our fame as lushes after all. And besides, I was treating the pain from the head wound Mr. Antsy Underpants had given me with a cold Tom Collins.

John Huston was no good at interviews, and this type of attention was a nuisance for him. Turning his back on the pesky reporters, he crossed in three long strides to the other side of the set, where his friend Guillermo Wolf, the engineer, was waiting for him. He was a chubby man. Robust but agile. The kind who'd run you over before you even got a look at the license plate. It was Wolf who'd convinced the great director to film a movie someplace as out of the way as Mismaloya in the first place.

Now Wolf looked upset. He talked in rapid English peppered with dirty Spanish. Huston just quietly nodded his head. Both men were chain smokers, nervously lighting the next cigarette before finishing the previous one. Wolf's diatribe had ended and Huston punctuated it with an expletive before returning to the group of journalists. This time it only took him two strides.

A copy of *Siempre!* landed on the bar in front of me. Stark threw a few copies of the *Los Angeles Times* on top of it. Then he added some gossip rags to the pile. They were all talking about us.

"Beautiful, Pascal," he exclaimed.

"I was in the wrong place at the wrong time. Story of my life."

"Today someone's coming in from Paris to interview John," Stark said. "In Europe everyone's talking about the new Sodom and Gomorrah on the Mexican Pacific. I like it." He squeezed my hand hard before leaving to give more interviews. Plenty of interviews.

My naïveté hurt worse than my head. I applied more Tom Collins to the wound. Stark's game wasn't hard to follow: free publicity, invaluable if you're an indie. How could I have been so stupid!

"He must really like you, but I don't think you're my type after all, honey," Gorman said as he sat down. This time he was wearing a knit blouse with so many stripes it looked like a TV with bad reception.

"And what is your type, genius?"

"The kind who prefer staying out of trouble. I make like I'm working, and they pay me for it."

"Lovely. Next time I'll scout for gossip and you take the beating."

"I don't think they'll crack you, honey. Your head is harder to bust open than a walnut," he said, flashing me a game-show-host smile.

"With all you've heard, is there anything I'd be interested in hearing?"

"Perhaps. And with all you've drunk, is there anything I'd be interested in drinking?"

Gorman was taking advantage of the situation, but he was worth the trouble. He could fill you in on Ava Gardner's shoe size. Or whether Richard Burton was as good a lover as Taylor bragged he was. Or even when Sue Lyon got her period.

"Tom Collins," I told the bartender.

"For one of those, I just might let it slip that the production is experiencing financial difficulties."

"But they've got a contract with Mr. Huston's friend," I replied. "They supply three squares a day and keep the drinks coming. So far, I can't see anything to complain about."

"Well, maybe next time Mr. Burton orders his bottle, they'll be fresh out…"

He threw me a kiss and marched off, scripts in one hand and cocktail in the other.

"By the way, *macho*, Miss Lyon wants to see you. She's in her dressing room," he added, almost as an afterthought.

XII

LOLITA

1½ OUNCES TEQUILA

¼ OUNCE LIME JUICE

1 TEASPOON HONEY

3–4 DASHES ANGOSTURA BITTERS

Mix together all the ingredients in an ice-filled shaker to the tone of "(There's) Always Something There to Remind Me" by Sandie Shaw, and strain over a couple of ice cubes into a cocktail glass.

Lolita *is the controversial novel by Vladimir Nabokov centering on the relationship between an adolescent nymphet and the middle-aged protagonist, Humbert Humbert. Published in the 1950s,* Lolita *became a near-instant classic, and a film by director Stanley Kubrick soon followed in 1962.*

This cocktail was said to be created by some sailors in a bar in the south of France. One can imagine the inspiration for the name probably owes more to the photo on the wall of Sue Lyon in a bikini than to the literary tastes of the regulars.

The bungalow that served as Sue Lyon's dressing room faced the ocean. It teetered on a rocky outcropping, like a full tray balanced by a waiter at a wedding. The roof tiles were made of red ceramic, and it was crowned by a set of useless wrought-iron ornaments that were supposed to look Mexican.

I stopped just outside the door, on a terrace sweetened by bougainvillea and colorful flowers. Music seeped through the open window. It was a song I'd heard on the radio several times. It was vying for first place on the hit parade against a foursome of snot-nosed brats from Liverpool. The song ended, and after a few clicks and clacks from the record player, it started playing again. Sue Lyon may be a famous actress, but she was still a teenager who enjoyed listening to hit songs on the radio.

"If she plays that song one more time, I'll have to shoot her with the pistol John gave me," a voice from behind whispered. It was a voice not meant to be heard from far away. Just a few inches from your pillow. Raspy, but exciting somehow.

It seemed to come from a hammock just underneath a palm tree nearby. My eyes had adjusted to the shade by the time I came to a halt beside her. She was the most beautiful creature in the world. Quite a bit of mileage on her, but well driven. One of the best-built chassis in Hollywood. And she knew it. To have been courted by many rich and famous men had given her a unique complacency. Her face had huge, deep, dark eyes, a firm jaw, the kind that doesn't dent when you kiss it hard, and lips the texture of fine silk. Costly silk.

Ava Gardner was wearing a dark blue cotton robe. Maybe she had on a bathing suit underneath. Maybe not.

"If I kill her, would you arrest me, Mr. Security Man?" she said, that last bit hot enough to melt vanilla ice cream.

"No," I managed, suddenly nervous. "My job would be the opposite: to make sure no one arrests you, Miss Gardner, so that when the filming's over you can go back to Madrid without a scratch, not even on your passport."

"Yes, yes, I know," she answered heartlessly. She smoked her cigarette despotically. There wasn't much room left in that chassis for a sense of humor. And if there was, it was being saved for whoever could pay for it.

"Would you like me to say something to Miss Lyon about her taste in music?" I replied as professionally as possible, considering the fact that I had Ava Gardner in a bathrobe right in front of me.

"Leave her alone. That girl's gonna need a hundred lovers and two thousand martinis before she understands the ways of the world. No doubt she'll end up living with some criminal. But tell her that once I lose my temper, I have a hard time finding it."

The cigarette smoke dispelled any angelic aura she might have still possessed. In fact, it made her look rather malevolent.

"Is there anything I can do for you?" I tried to play nice.

"Sure, you can go find all those weasels looking for their hundred-dollar snapshot and put a bullet into each and every one of them. They only invent affairs and romances in order to sell more magazines. Can you believe what they're saying about me and that brute of an *indio*, Fernández?"

"Sorry. I don't read magazines; they insult my stupidity."

"They say I kissed him."

"And did you?"

"Kid, everybody kisses everybody else in this disgusting business. It's the kissiest line of work in the world."

I smiled. I'd gotten a laugh out of her for free. Others would pay thousands. Her eyes were boring right through me, but I didn't move.

"Aren't they expecting you in there?" She said languidly, as if she were about to fall asleep.

The conversation was over. And I had to admit it hadn't been my smoothest encounter with a movie star. I turned around and headed back to Lyon's bungalow.

The same song was still playing. I stuck my head through the open door. The place looked empty, but there was a strong smell of ocean and sex. An aroma so sweet, they should bottle it and sell it as this summer's fragrance.

"Hello," I called out.

A bare torso appeared from behind the sofa. He gave me a "who, me?" look: Bugs Bunny caught stealing carrots. Lyon popped up next to him, her bra halfway off. I could see one of her egg-shaped breasts, her nipple a tiny yolk.

"Just a minute," she managed to say between giggles.

I ducked back outside. While I waited for the lovebirds to change out of their Adam and Eve costumes and into something more suitable for the movie set, my gaze sought out Gardner. The hammock was empty. She hadn't even given me the pleasure of seeing her shins.

"Please come in," Lyon said in the schoolgirl voice she had down pat.

Lyon was sitting in the living room. On a table before her rested a bottle of tequila and two marijuana joints, unsmoked. She reached for one, then made an old Zippo lighter—the one I'd already seen in Blondie's hands—screech. She breathed in the flame and exhaled a thread of smoke, then passed it to me without saying a word. Her boyfriend was buttoning up his shirt and running his fingers through his hair, which stubbornly stood up on end. I guessed her mother wasn't in.

"He's not one of us," her boyfriend said with a nauseated expression from the other side of the room.

I made the same face back at him and took the joint from Lyon's fingers, gave it a big pull, and held the smoke until I could feel it invading my throat. Then I exhaled, reaching for the bottle of tequila on the table.

"You called me. Here I am," I said, taking a swig right out of the bottle, without taking my eyes off the boyfriend. He saw I wasn't going to play his little game, lost interest, and picked up a magazine.

"Forget it, Sue. He doesn't understand what it means to be famous. I'm already an actor, and I'm going to direct a film just to get rid of losers like him."

"Yeah, he acted in a film," Lyon said. "He played one of the zombies."

"Nominated for the Oscar, no doubt."

The boyfriend didn't turn around. Either he hadn't heard me or decided not to listen. He continued paging through his magazine.

"I'd like to thank you for what you did for Eva," Lolita whispered.

"It was nothing. But I won't be able to hold off the police for long. They can get annoying with all their silly questions about drugs, or about the guy who got away. I don't have enough hush money for all that."

This last phrase made Lyon's eyes open so wide they almost popped out of her head.

"She's already spoken to the chief of police. They drugged her and kidnapped her. It was a miracle you were able to save her in time," she said.

"Some people call me Sir Lancelot. I'm a knight in shining armor on Saturdays, Sundays, and days off."

"She's a good teacher," she continued. "She's expanded my mind. She knows a lot and has traveled a lot. She's not a piece of shit like all the rest. She won't let Hollywood ruin me like it has Liz and Deborah."

"Yeah, it's really crummy that they're famous and earn millions of dollars. Someone oughta get the electric chair." I was taking it out on her, but it was Blondie who deserved my sarcasm. "If you want to ruin your life, you don't need Hollywood's help, young lady. You're already well on your way."

To her surprise, I abruptly stood up. Hampton Fancher ran toward me, full of bravado.

"You're being disrespectful to Sue. That's gonna hurt."

He telegraphed his attack. I used the same punch that the Indian, Fernández, had used on me: in the face, right between the eyes.

Fancher went flying over the sofa and landed on the coffee table. The tequila and joints floated in midair until gravity did its part. I was expecting a scream or at least some tears from Lyon, but her jaw just dropped. Another dumb blonde to swell the ranks of Movieland.

"Is Eva okay?" I asked in a conciliatory fashion.

Lyon answered, completely ignoring the curses coming from her boyfriend, who was trying to get to his feet.

"Yes. Actually she's been asking for you."

"Tell her something nice, something she'd like. On my behalf."

I walked out, mentally erasing Sue Lyon from future sexual fantasies.

XIII

WHITE RUSSIAN

2 PARTS VODKA

1 PART COFFEE LIQUEUR, PREFERABLY KAHLÚA

MILK OR LIGHT CREAM

*B*lend the vodka, chilled if possible, with the coffee liqueur. Serve in a short glass with ice. Slowly add the milk or cream to taste in order to achieve an appealing visual effect.

A cocktail for many occasions, the White Russian is named in honor of the "anti-Bolsheviks," or supporters of the czar, from the 1917 Revolution. It isn't a Russian cocktail, but it is prepared with vodka. The Black Russian came first in the 1940s, and with the addition of cream sometime later became "white" and sweeter, and a particular hit with the ladies. Mix one up and turn on the sweet sounds of Eartha Kitt singing "C'est Si Bon" to the accompaniment of Henri René's orchestra.

The next day there was nothing more for me to do on the set. I went back to the hotel to get some shut-eye. With a little luck, my encounter with Sue and her hotheaded boyfriend would turn out to have been no more than a bad dream.

Two heavy knocks on the door woke me from my slumber. They must have been fairly hard, as up to now I'd been able to sleep right through the church bells next to my hotel. Coming to consciousness, I realized I'd fallen asleep in my street clothes and an empty bottle of gin was lying beside me. I would have preferred Blondie.

Again the pounding echoed in my ears like war drums. This time I was sure it could be heard all the way to China. Mao was probably wondering what in the hell was so urgent, too.

I stumbled toward the door. "Mr. Burton and Miss Taylor wanna see you," a voice said in clumsy English, as rough as a Harlem garbage dump.

Standing before me was the largest man I'd ever seen. On his neck he carried something vaguely similar to a head. Big face, snub nose so broad it looked like the prow on a cruise ship, and eyes ridiculously small in comparison with his long, almost girlish eyelashes. His chest was enormous, like a Sherman tank, and I was sure his knuckles touched the floor. He wore a tight sport shirt, short pants, and tennis shoes that made him look like an orangutan outfitted for Wimbledon. Only the orangutan would have been better looking. His hand, so broad I could have pulled up and sat down on it, grabbed me by the shoulder and pulled me out of the room in one swift motion.

"Mr. Burton and Miss Taylor wanna see you," he repeated in the same tone.

"I heard you already. Got any other sentences? Or did your record get scratched?" I answered. My feet were dangling several inches above the floor by this point, but my question must have thrown him off, because he dropped me. I took advantage of the opportunity and stepped quickly back inside the room.

"Are you Sunny Pascal?" he growled.

"Only when it suits me."

This time he was thoughtful, not knowing what to do.

I was starting to like our little exchange. It gave me enough time to clean myself up while the big ape reflected on his bananas. A final look in the mirror assured me that I was presentable enough for an audience with the famous couple and headed back over to King Kong.

"You said it."

"What did I say?" he asked me, scratching his head.

"Mr. Burton and Miss Taylor wanna see me. After you."

For the first time, he saw the light and gave me a goofy grin that was short one tooth. I couldn't help thinking he looked like a fat kid who'd just been given a piece of candy.

This fat kid had one nice ride, I'll give him that. A beautiful Cadillac convertible waited outside the Rio Hotel. I barely managed to get in before King Kong took off like a madman, hitting every pothole in Vallarta. Two dogs and a donkey almost met their maker as we careened up the vertiginous streets. At least they would have died with class: this was one exquisite car.

We reached a cobblestoned street in the upper part of town. The river ran along one side, murmuring peacefully. King Kong parked the car across from an enormous white facade with ashlar masonry. The entrance was protected by a huge mango tree brimming with fruit just waiting to drop on unwary pedestrians. A few mangos lay smashed on the ground, and the sickly sweet odor of fermented fruit crept into my nostrils.

An elegantly lettered sign made of ceramic tiles read "Kimberly House."

King Kong placed his hand on my shoulder and propelled me through the entryway. There among the flowers and bougainvillea, two boys and a little girl played at splashing each other with buckets of water. They were lovely children, blonde and blue eyed, the kind only a gorgeous woman can produce.

Under the shade of a tile roof, a room filled with rustic leather-and-pine furniture sprawled like a retired tourist. There Elizabeth Taylor reclined in her trademark Cleopatra pose. She was dressed in a long white tunic, open at the side to display a burnished, well-defined leg. Her hair was gathered back in a great bow. In her hand, she held what looked like a White Russian. A nearly empty box of chocolates lay to one side. A large pair of dark glasses shaded her famous violet-colored eyes. Her equally famous cleavage was crowned by an enormous collar of stones so ridiculously large, they could have passed for costume jewelry. She indeed looked like a queen—much better, in fact, than the sourpuss on the British pound.

A small bar with bottles of every shape and size stood like an altar at the far end of the room. At the center, instead of the parish priest, however, was Richard Burton in a tight bathing suit and a wide linen shirt. He looked more relaxed than he had on the set, almost paternal.

"You're the sleuth, right?" Burton asked me in his distinctive Welsh accent. "I've seen you on the set. You're hard to beat."

"I think you've already won, and I don't even know what we're playing. I couldn't hope to match what I see here, Mr. Burton."

He roared with laughter. One of the children turned around, mocking him. Taylor didn't so much as look at me; she wasn't taking her eyes off the children. Like a lioness watching her cubs play with a rattlesnake.

"Drinks. I meant drinks," he explained. "Between the two of us, we're going to bankrupt Stark. Our bar tab is going to cost him more than the goddamned film." He raised a bottle without a label. The contents were as pure as the diamonds nestled on his girlfriend's breast. "Raicilla?"

"Only if you're driving. They took away my license."

He roared again. None of the children turned around this time. He poured two tall shot glasses and passed one to me. He waited until my fingers had grazed the glass, and then he knocked his back in one swallow. I didn't want to fall behind; mine disappeared just as quickly.

"This raicilla is good for the soul. You can feel how it trickles down into your gut." He took a seat on one of the chairs and refilled the glasses. "I've been talking to the Indians who sell it to me. They make it out of local maguey. It has a little mescaline, like peyote. That's why it makes you feel so light."

"Better than anesthesia."

"I ought to bottle it and sell it in the States. I'd become more of a millionaire than any bloody Hollywood actor." Again the laugh. Not even Liz turned her head. It seems British humor is as odd as steering wheels on the right and drinking tea in the middle of the afternoon.

"We have a delicate matter to discuss. John said you might be able to help us," he murmured seriously.

"As long as we don't have to kill anybody. I don't like bloodstains on my clothes. They're hard to wash out."

"Liz lost something. Something she holds in high regard. We'd like to recover it…" He turned to her. She rewarded him with the gaze of a cat about to pounce. "Of course, I don't mean her acting career. That would be no small feat, after our leading roles in *Cleopatra*. We wouldn't want to die in the attempt." This time it was my turn to laugh. The Brit had the acid humor of a drunk who has just got run over by a bicycle.

"It's a gold ring, set with rubies and pearls," Taylor said, interrupting our little chat. "The king of Indonesia gave it to me." Her voice was hard and sweet, like a good slap after a soft kiss.

"I'm marrying Liz for her jewels. The only thing I've got to offer in exchange is me…which is more than enough for any woman." Taylor gave him a hard punch in the stomach while he laughed. I was expecting them to take out the gold pistols John Huston had given them and open fire.

"It disappeared from the house last night," Miss Taylor concluded.

"Well, I don't think they'll try to sell it in town. Selling the Statue of Liberty in the Sahara Desert would be more subtle. Your ring is no doubt on its way to Mexico City, ma'am."

"No, it's still here in town." Burton turned toward his friendly giant, who was still standing there beside him, and said, "Bobby, show him the note."

King Kong disappeared into another room, then reappeared with a white envelope and placed it clumsily into my hands.

Inside the envelope was a folded sheet. A sum of money was written on it, and an address: "Salado Bridge. Midnight. No cops." I folded it again and put it back into the envelope. Who knows, maybe they wanted to keep it as a Mexican souvenir.

"Smart. They know what they're doing. If they'd tried to run, Interpol would've tracked them out of the country."

"Money is not an issue. We just want you to accompany Bobby to the drop-off. You know about these things. Our bodyguard, here, is just an ex-boxer."

I turned to look at the giant, who returned another gap-toothed grin. I adored him even more.

"Do you want me to apprehend them?"

"We don't want any shooting, or for you to play the hero. We don't want any more publicity than we already have. Liz is doing the paperwork to divorce Eddie Fisher, and I'm working on mine with Sue, right here in Puerto Vallarta. This might make the local authorities nervous. Come back with the ring and you'll be handsomely rewarded."

"I'm on Mr. Stark's payroll. It's my job," I said and then added, "Another glass of raicilla should settle the score."

Burton turned to look at his future wife. She folded herself on the sofa while scolding one of her children for wallowing in the garden.

Burton poured me another raicilla. I guess we had a deal.

XIV

SIDECAR

2 OUNCES BRANDY

1 OUNCE LEMON JUICE

1 OUNCE COINTREAU OR TRIPLE SEC

SUGAR

*B*lend and chill with ice. Serve in a cocktail glass with a sugared rim. "Makin' Whoopee" by Ella Fitzgerald perfectly reflects this drink's prewar esprit.*

According to David A. Embury, renowned cocktail historian, the sidecar was invented by a World War I captain who stopped in a Paris bar, hoping for a daiquiri. The bar was out of rum, so he had to settle for brandy instead, and the sidecar was born. The new drink needed a name, and "sidecar" seemed fitting, since the bar's owner was known for riding a motorcycle equipped with one.

Bobby La Salle was Richard Burton's bodyguard, trainer, and Ping-Pong opponent. Burton's agent and Liz Taylor's ex, Michael Wilding, had hired him. I asked Bobby Gorilla whether Wilding had enough guts to shine his ex-wife's shoes, but Bobby didn't get it; you couldn't hold a complex conversation with him any more than you could with a child.

Burton handed me another envelope, this one stuffed with crisp, clean hundred-dollar bills. It was a sum I figured I'd never come across again in my lifetime, even if I robbed a bank. The Welshman downed a few more drinks with us as we waited for nightfall.

When the time had come, I asked Bobby to take me to my hotel first. Burton had said no guns, but I had learned long ago that you didn't walk around with that kind of money without some backup. Bobby was a good start, but my Colt was more trustworthy and less bulky.

On our way to the hotel, Bobby told me about his glory days as a boxer, and I told him about my interest in surfing. He wanted to be an actor now, and I cheered him on. After all he was as goofy as a cartoon character, and everybody likes them.

The church bells tolled midnight as we headed out on the highway toward the city limits. There wasn't much traffic, just a few tractor trailers on their way to Guadalajara.

The moon reflected on the surface of the sea, and the palm trees swayed in the night breeze, which was perfumed with the salty smell of seaweed. We crossed the Salado River, and the Cadillac turned inland. The land on both sides of us was overrun by jungle, and all we could hear were the songs of crickets and toads. At a clearing by the river, where some fishing boats rested on the bank alongside their extended nets, I killed the motor. The crickets and toads grew louder. It seemed deserted enough, but you could probably have hidden a German tank in the undergrowth if you wanted to.

"We're in the middle of nowhere. Here, even the lizards get bored," I told Bobby, as a few frogs splashed into the water, reminding us that we were not completely alone.

A flashlight beam shone in our eyes. It came from a leafy tree not more than thirty feet from the car. I felt like a deer caught in headlights.

"Stay in the car. I'll take care of this," Bobby Gorilla said, grabbing the envelope of money. He got out of the car and raised both hands in the air. I managed to discern a shape behind the beam of light. It approached the former boxer. Their voices merged with the noise of the river and its inhabitants, and I couldn't make out more than a word here and there.

The crickets and toads finally took five, and I was able to hear the man with the flashlight say, "Did you bring the money, *cabrón*?"

It was spoken in a fast and zesty Spanish. Not the kind spoken on the coasts but city Spanish. Professional, criminal Spanish.

I didn't want Burton to have the impression that all Mexicans were a bunch of crooks. I had to do something, so I slowly drew my Colt from my shoulder holster and climbed out of the car. I didn't care anymore if my baby caught cold. There'd be time enough for it to recover.

"*Dinero* here, *anillo.*" Bobby articulated the two Spanish words I'd taught him on the way over. I heard a grunt. Voices. Arguing.

A shot.

This was getting interesting. It certainly wasn't the crickets or toads who'd fired. The ones packing the weapons were another kind of vermin. I heard Bobby cursing, spewing words I am sure his mother wouldn't want to hear. I released the safety.

Another shot.

Two shots are too many for one night. Before I could move a muscle, a finger touched my shoulder. Then the barrel of a gun. I can still remember the words whispered in my ear before I fell unconscious, "This is for hurting my arm." Call it a drunkard's intuition, but I knew that voice belonged to Mr. Antsy Underpants.

XV

BLUE LAGOON

1 OUNCE VODKA

1 OUNCE BLUE CURAÇAO

7 OUNCES LEMONADE

1 MARASCHINO CHERRY

*B*lend vodka, curaçao, and lemonade with ice. May be enjoyed with rum and Malibu coconut cream, or sweetened with sugar. Garnish with the cherry and the tunes of Mel Tormé.

The blue lagoon was created by Andy MacElhone, a famous bartender and son of the owner of Harry's New York Bar in Paris. The drink was named after the 1949 film directed by Frank Launder and based on a Victorian romance by the novelist Henry De Vere Stacpoole. Years later, in 1980, a new version of the movie was released, making actress Brooke Shields famous.

I was somewhat dizzy when I came to and suffering my worst hangover ever.

"You're an irresponsible drunk. Did you think your old man would be proud of someone like you?"

I could hear voices speaking to me in the dark, but I couldn't make out a face.

"It's my life. I'm not you."

"Tough guy, huh?"

"They're my mistakes. Don't fuck with me…"

I dragged myself across the wet ground and managed to get up on one knee. The voices continued, but they were only in my head. I was alone. Steadying myself with both hands, I tried to stand but fell down again, my hands covered with wet sand.

Slowly coming to my senses, I tried again. The second attempt was painful but successful. I got up with all the caution of an ice skater who's just fallen flat on his ass, using the trunk-door handle for support. My joints were still numb.

I lifted one hand to my head. It felt as swollen and soft as a ripe mango. Having already kicked me once before in the jaw, Mr. Antsy Underpants had added another blow to the base of my skull this time. Running my fingers through my hair, I felt a sticky wetness. My head was bleeding freely.

My eyes focused on a large shape in front of me. It was the Cadillac. I stumbled over to it, opened the door, and collapsed in the driver's seat. The keys were still in the ignition. I just sat there like a putz, the prize champion of putzes. For a second it occurred to me I should lay off the bottle. But just for a second, before I convinced myself that what I really needed was another shot of that raicilla.

Where Bobby had been standing there was only darkness. I heard a man groaning in pain among the crickets and a motor purring in the distance. Headlights fell on the Cadillac and the clearing around us. I could see Bobby's body lying a few feet away.

If the headlights belonged to the same guys that had done that to Bobby, there'd be no escape. I felt for my Colt. It was gone. The approaching headlights grew brighter.

The car stopped in front of me, blinding me for a second time that night. I could see it was a convertible jeep. A war relic. A Napoleonic soldier would have been more modern and better equipped. My intuition told me there'd be no trouble from that jalopy.

With enormous effort, I pulled myself out of the car and stumbled toward the ex-boxer. Bobby was alive and moaning, but I could see he was about to pass out. A bullet had gone through his thigh. Nothing to worry about. What a shame it would have been for the world to lose a future star like him, I thought. He'd received the same blow to the head, or maybe two, as I had, enough to knock him out at least. There was a lot of blood beside him, but none of it appeared to be his; it was nowhere near his leg wound.

A shadow blocked the headlights all of a sudden. I turned and gazed into the blinding halo of light. A robust but hunched silhouette appeared. I could see it wore shorts and a scruffy beard. I don't know which I recognized first, his voice or the smell of his T-shirt.

"*Soldado*, next time better invite me to the party. *Más diversión* than a cantina, huh?"

Billy Joe, my drinking buddy from Mazatlán, kneeled down beside me and started tending to Bobby La Salle.

"Your amigo needs a doctor. He's not hurt bad, but he could still bleed to death."

The old man lifted the boxer like a sack of potatoes and dragged him over to his jeep, depositing him in the backseat with all the delicacy of an airport luggage handler.

"Compadre, you look *muy mal*. Let me see that wound."

I bent my head down so the old man could take a closer look. He gave a long whistle and moved away from me, as if my head wound and bad luck might be contagious. Leaning against the bumper of the jeep, he raised one of his British cigarettes to his lips and lit it, then offered me one.

"No thanks. They're bad for your health."

"Just like your line of work, *soldado*." He took a deep drag and gave me the same smile he'd offered before, like Santa Claus having been asked for an impossible gift. Goddamned Santa. "You drive the Cadillac," he said.

"What about the money?" I asked.

"Your amigo's clean."

"No. He was carrying an envelope with cash. I guess our date didn't feel like giving up the ring. They must have kept the ransom money."

"Rings, money, and a kick in head. *Mucho bueno* work."

"So how come you show up out here in the middle of nowhere, mister?" I asked. "And I don't like your half-assed whorish answers anymore. If you tell me you're out here hunting lizards, I swear I'll do you worse than they did Bobby."

"I followed your trail from town. *Esta ser carretera*, the road, for cheap *putas* there. I saw your lights. It's too cold to be a couple screwing…"

"I wouldn't know. Haven't noticed any this trip," I replied. My head had finally stopped buzzing. Now it was just pain I felt. "Rescued by an old wise guy. Sergeant Quintero's gonna love hearing this one."

"Billy Joe's always *listo, soldado*," he said, getting into his car. "Follow me. Don't die on the way, *por favor*. I still want *putas baratas*."

"You're the champion jokester, mister," I replied, my head still aching. I got back into the Cadillac and started the ignition. It took all my concentration not to drive off the road, though before reaching Puerto Vallarta, I did have to stop and throw up, making a terrible mess in the Cadillac. It was all that raicilla I'd drunk with Richard Burton. I was simply returning the favor.

XVI

NEGRONI

1 PART GIN

1 PART CAMPARI

1 PART SWEET VERMOUTH

1 LEMON TWIST

*S*hake the gin, Campari, and vermouth with ice to chill. Strain into a cocktail glass with a few ice cubes, and garnish with the lemon twist.

The negroni hails from Florence, Italy, and was invented in the early twenties in honor of Count Camillo Negroni, who asked a bartender to add gin instead of soda water to his favorite cocktail, the Americano. The negroni didn't make its debut in the United States until 1947, however. Here's a cocktail to whet your appetite while Sammy Davis Jr. sings "The Girl from Ipanema."

Just as I'd thought, Sergeant Quintero loved my story. In his own reserved way, he was whooping and bouncing off the walls. Very much in his own way: he raised one eyebrow and said in his standard bored tone of voice, *"Mis huevos."*

Of course, I spiced it up a bit. Like when you inherit a recipe. You add a little something, you take a little something out. And you always season to taste: Bobby La Salle and I were out practicing our aim, using river lizards as targets. That night there must have been a Rotary Club meeting or something, because there were no lizards to shoot. Then a gang of ruffians attacked us. It was highway robbery. It was a miracle I wasn't killed. I would have been too, if not for the boxer's courage. While trying to defend me, he took a bullet in the leg. The criminals took off, leaving a cloud of dust behind. Maybe they were late for that Rotary Club meeting. They left us in a sorry state: food for their colleagues, the lizards. Billy Joe had heard the shots and decided to investigate. And that's how he found us.

At least I didn't lie about cheap whores.

"Mis huevos," Quintero repeated.

Bobby lowered his head. He had a bandage that made him look like a gift-wrapped coconut. Another bandage covered the wound on his leg. He'd gotten off easy: only five stitches. It had cost me seven on the nape of the neck. They hurt more than the first kick in the nuts you get in grade school.

Billy Joe smiled, using that Santa Claus expression of his. Goddamned Santa.

"The *muchacho* tells the truth. Drunk sailors, maybe." With that, the old man was done. It was like adorning Quintero's drink with a paper umbrella to see if he'd swallow it whole.

The old man smoked one of his cigarettes. Quintero, not wanting to be left out, removed a package of cheap, filterless Alas from his ridiculous blue shirt. Between the two of them, they puffed more smoke than a broken-down truck. Bobby Gorilla coughed. I liked the fact that he didn't smoke; he was a true athlete.

"Mr. Rogue, it's been a long time since you gave us any trouble. Do you really want to stick your nose into this and end up with blood on your hands because of this pair of *pendejos*?"

It surprised me that our friendly local Puerto Vallarta police officer was capable of articulating such a phrase; maybe he had gone to school after all, maybe even junior high.

"Sergeant, that bells thing was Manuel's goddamned idea." I must have looked confused, because Billy Joe turned to explain. "Arrested by the police the other night. Got drunk with *cabrón* Manuel Lepe. We went to ring church bells."

"At four in the morning," Quintero added in an annoyed tone. I tried to contain myself, but the image of that old man playing childish pranks—like peeping at girls in the bathroom or placing a tack on a chair or ringing church bells in the middle of the night—made me laugh out loud.

I'd met Manuel Lepe on one of my drunken sprees: he was a local *artiste*, a well-known character in town, who'd devoted himself to painting canvases that looked like gorgeous pipe dreams: infantile drawings of children, little donkeys, birds; everybody grinning and flying around like angels. Heroin doesn't generally provide such pleasant visions.

"It'd all be beautiful if it weren't for the fact that we picked up a stiff," Quintero told us sadly, like a bad actor on a Mexican soap opera. "In the river, a few feet away from where you were. It was thrown off the bridge and ran aground alongside the highway. Lucky the current was slow."

"And does this body have a name?" I asked. Naïveté is the best weapon against cops.

"Believe it or not, it does. A guy called José Antonio Contreras. From Mexico City. A real luxury model: wanted for murder, robbery, and beating up bunny rabbits on Sundays. Suspected in the infamous killing of Mercedes Cassola and Ycilio Massine, and a known member of gangs run by Carlos Zippo, Giuseppe Bari, and the Nava."

"This can't be for real. You're making those names up," I said with a smile.

"Sure. Just like the stiff."

"No big loss. Maybe just some poor brokenhearted soul who jumped off the bridge," I concluded, trying to wrap up this mess.

"Sure, the kind of suicide you only find in Mexico—with a bullet in the chest. A little present from one of you, perhaps?" Quintero asked.

Silence. The street noise had suddenly died. Even the goddamned crickets awaited our answer.

"It wasn't us," I protested, breaking the awful silence. "I was packing my Colt. It didn't so much as cough." The crickets started chirping again. "And how did you find out so much about a dead guy in less than an hour?" I added. "Even James Bond would be impressed by the Vallarta police force." I've found that playing the funny guy also helps with cops. Especially when they're pointing a gun at you.

"We were already after this dude. His gang specialized in jewel theft. Our snitch said he was working for Bernabé Jurado here in town. With all these tourists, Puerto Vallarta is a thieves' paradise."

He looked us up and down, like three kids getting scolded at recess. And then he must have decided to take pity on us. "Get outta here," he barked, "before I find a reason to lock you up all week."

"No *problemo, soldado*. Though the coffee in jail is better than at the Hotel Rosita," Billy Joe had to add. That really put Quintero in a bad mood. He cursed a blue streak as he escorted us out to the street.

XVII

MOJITO

2-3 OUNCES RUM

JUICE FROM 1 LIME

2 TABLESPOONS SUGAR

2-4 SPEARMINT LEAVES

2-3 OUNCES SODA WATER

*C*rush the mint leaves to release their flavor. Add the sugar and lime juice, and stir until you can smell the mint. Then pour into a highball glass with the rum and ice, and top off with the soda water.

The mojito made its appearance in the early twentieth century at Mariano Beach, a popular Cuban resort. But the drink didn't become famous until Angel Martinez opened La Bodeguita del Medio. Ernest Hemingway discovered mojitos in this famous restaurant during his years in Havana, where he continued to live even after the revolution, no doubt so he could keep savoring this delicious concoction. The drink won over other famous people like Brigitte Bardot, Pablo Neruda, Nat King Cole, and Errol Flynn, all of whom enjoyed it with "Maracaibo."

———————

I couldn't face Kimberly House and Richard Burton just yet. I didn't want to explain how his money had gone up in smoke. But Bobby La Salle didn't have a choice. He told me that since I'd covered for him with the cops, he'd return the favor. He was a nice enough critter. You just had to keep him well fed.

He dropped me and Billy Joe off at the Rio Hotel.

The bartender was wearily presiding over a group of journalists from Chicago who were getting progressively drunker. Billy Joe paid the man for a round of mojitos and offered him such a healthy tip he was able to close up shop and call it a night. The journalists fell asleep at their table while we drank our mojitos.

"How did you get to be a bloodhound, *soldado*?" the old man asked me, point-blank.

"That's a long story."

"This time of night, I won't find my *barata* whores, so I've got time."

He was right. No whores for him and no Blondie for me; she was probably counting opium sheep by now. The old man and I would have to keep each other company.

"I was sixteen when I left my mother's house," I said. "Nothing personal. I just couldn't spend my life attending family reunions on Saturday and mass on Sunday. It's against my religion."

I didn't usually feel comfortable talking about myself. Bloodhounds don't do that; they just provide sarcastic back talk. That's why they're tough guys. But the events of the evening must have had an impact because I couldn't shut up.

"I thought I'd be better off with my father. Everything was fine until I hit him back. At least the blood stayed in the family: mine on his fists and his in my mouth."

"*Hermoso*."

"An old LA detective, Michael Carmandy, hired me. He'd been a private dick during Prohibition, one of the best. A loner and heavy drinker who couldn't be bought off. By then he was already a brand name. He had ten assistants and three secretaries, one of whom was a doll, beautiful, in fact."

"Your first heartbreak?"

"No, just irreconcilable differences. She wanted kids, a house in San Diego, and a vacation home in Acapulco. I wanted booze, fun, and recreational drugs. When she married an architect from Chicago—a Mexican to boot—I quit. Carmandy recommended me to his contacts."

"You like him more than your father?"

"Mussolini would have been better than my dad." I ended my story abruptly, closing the curtain on that act. "Now I work for myself. Pays for my vices and the rent."

"A real winner."

I didn't like the old man's comment. I didn't like his smile either. But I really didn't like my own life story.

Billy Joe and I retreated to my room. The bar had been closed for so long, the journalists were already snoring. I was certain that one of my bottles of gin still had something to offer. It was already three in the morning; the night couldn't get any worse.

I was wrong. It got worse. It looked like a hurricane had touched down in my room. Although a hurricane wouldn't have been so rough. One of my surfboards was even broken in two. Billy Joe was more upset to see the broken bottle of gin, though.

My clothes were such a mess it looked like the floor of my studio in Venice Beach, but at least there I would have known where everything was. Whoever did this did it with feeling. This had the stench of Mr. Antsy Underpants all over it.

I could just imagine him enjoying this little remodel.

"This wasn't vengeance. You've got something. That's why he didn't kill you at the river," Billy Joe declared.

"I have nothing of value," I said. "I always carry everything with me, and I already lost the Colt Carmandy gave me earlier tonight."

"You've got something," Billy Joe repeated, lighting one of his British cigarettes.

I looked at the mess, annoyed. What little was mine was there. Unless, of course, they were looking for something that wasn't mine.

"The roll of film," I exclaimed. "The one I found at the house. I kept it because I didn't want the cops to see it. Because of the girl's mother."

The old man gave me a knowing look, like someone who can tell you how the movie ends before he even enters the theater. Goddamned Santa.

"I'm going to sleep. Next time you got a date and need a good rifle, call me," he said.

I wished him a very good evening and told him to dream of sweet little angels, like the kind Manuel Lepe paints.

XVIII

DAIQUIRI

2 OUNCES WHITE RUM

JUICE FROM 2 LIMES

1 TEASPOON SUGAR

10 DROPS MARASCHINO LIQUEUR

1 ORANGE SLICE

*M*ix the rum, lime juice, sugar, and maraschino liqueur *with ice in a cocktail shaker. If you prefer it frappé, mix in an electric blender. Serve in a wide glass garnished with the slice of orange. Then form a conga line and dance to the beat of Desi Arnaz's hit tune "Babalu."*

The daiquiri is actually a whole family of cocktails, with its primary ingredients being rum and lime juice. There are as many kinds as there are fruit flavors, but the version that gained international fame was born in one of the most famous bars in the world: El Floridita in Havana, Cuba.

Daiquiri is actually the name of a beach near Santiago, Cuba, where a steel mill is located. They say a US engineer, Jennings

Cox, invented the first one, giving it the simple moniker of "natural daiquiri." It was later perfected by Constantino Ribalaigua Vert, bartender and owner of El Floridita, and the joint came to be known as the "Daiquiri Palace." Ernest Hemingway dubbed it the "Great Constant" after tasting Ribalaigua Vert's version. The daiquiri continued to gain popularity through the decades, even inside the White House, where it was rumored to be John F. Kennedy's favorite drink at mealtime.

The guy in charge of the hotel was nice enough to offer me another room. He didn't like the current decor in the old one either. I slept all day and all night, and when I woke up the next morning, my injuries hurt worse than before.

For breakfast, I ordered a couple of huevos rancheros, yolks intact; refried beans with a touch of sour cream; toast; and a pot of coffee from room service. I devoured it all.

Then I took a long, luxurious shower, like a debutante before her sweet-sixteen party.

The man I saw in the mirror when I stepped out of the shower looked a lot like me. He had the same face, but he looked roughed up, tired, and bruised like a melon. The visage made me queasy.

I dressed and decided I better get back to work. The motorboat took me across the water to Mismaloya.

Arriving fashionably late to roll call that day, I noticed nothing was any different than it had been. Everyone was hurrying around retrieving, transporting, or exchanging something. I crossed the set, headed for my usual seat at the bar, grateful Richard Burton wasn't in this scene. He'd be tied up for safekeeping at Kimberly House by his lioness, no doubt.

I ordered a daiquiri, testing our bartender's skill. It wasn't half bad, though I'd drunk better urine in public bathrooms. I settled into my seat, said a silent prayer to the selfish God to make Blondie appear, and drank.

Lately, that was what I did best: drink.

I could see John Huston chewing on a cigar the size of a thimble and hear that Gabriel Figueroa had decided on the opera *Mikado* for today's soundtrack. His Italian wasn't any better than his English, but his voice made the bottles on the bar tremble. For an opera singer, he was an excellent cinematographer.

Much to my disappointment, Blondie didn't show.

But I did spy a group of local Indians again, looking on in silence from the edge of the jungle. This time a family had gathered. The man was no older than I was, a sparse beard surrounding his mouth. The woman was pregnant and nursing a baby. Three children, mucus encrusted beneath their noses, were seated, resting. Their eyes were dark, deep, and hopeless.

My daydreaming was interrupted by a loud noise. The sound of objects creaking, then falling from high above. Noises that signal blood, pain, and maybe even death.

I saw members of the staff running toward one of the bungalows. I jumped from my seat, reached for my Colt, and then remembered I'd lost it.

One of the set balconies had collapsed, taking two assistants down with it. It didn't look promising: the balcony had fallen down the cliff between jagged rocks. Two men were trapped among the rubble a few yards away from the crashing waves. One of them was Tom Shaw, the assistant director. I didn't recognize the second man.

Tom looked worse off than his companion though. He tried to speak, but blood bubbled from his mouth. People were shouting, calling for help. All I could think was that we were a long way away from the beaten path, a long way for the Red Cross ambulances to come.

I shouted for a rope, and someone furnished one. Tying one end to a column and the other to my waist, and praying to the God of drunks that I'd live to taste one last martini, I descended down the cliff face.

Tom kept trying to call out as I moved carefully down the wall. His blood began staining the rocks, mixing with bird guano. Other men followed me down the rope. I reached the spot where he landed but was scared to move him. With the help of the others, I was able to carefully move him onto the waiting motorboat that would take him to Puerto Vallarta. The next motorboat, the one meant for his companion, was working its way toward shore.

I climbed back up the rope and returned to the scene of the accident. It was free of onlookers now. I could see the construction was of poor quality. The only way to win at this game was to do things on the cheap. But no matter how bad a job the builders had done, there was no reason for this building to have crumbled like a sand castle.

Bending down to study the remains hanging from the demolished terrace, I could see that the rods holding the beams had been cut with a hacksaw. This was no accident; someone had wanted blood.

"Goddamned Indians. They build everything out of sand," Huston grunted behind me.

I stood up and turned around. The director was only inches away; he could have easily shoved me off the precipice in this position. In fact, if he'd so much as exhaled, he would have. I swallowed hard. He was a full head taller than me.

Huston gave two chews to his cigar, regarding me silently. It was the kind of silence that comes after they hand down your sentence at a trial, or after she tells you she's pregnant. Then he just turned and walked away, grumbling, "By God! We better finish this goddamned film before we all end up swallowed alive by the jungle."

I found my breath again and quickly moved away from the edge of the construction, sure I'd wet myself.

XIX

MANHATTAN

2 OUNCES WHISKEY

½ OUNCE SWEET VERMOUTH

2–3 DASHES ANGOSTURA BITTERS

1 MARASCHINO CHERRY

Mix ingredients with ice in a shaker, blending until frosted. Serve in a cocktail glass. Garnish with the maraschino cherry. Drink while listening to "I'd Like to Hate Myself in the Morning" by Shirley Bassey.

The manhattan was first mixed in the late nineteenth century, when famous partygoer Jenny Jerome asked the bartender, during an animated event at the Manhattan Club, to serve something special to then New York governor Samuel J. Tilden. The cocktail became famous on Wall Street, Broadway, and in Hollywood during its golden age.

Filming was suspended for two days while all the buildings were thoroughly checked, so we all retreated to our respective hotels.

I was one of the last ones to catch transport to Puerto Vallarta. And by the time I arrived at the Rio Hotel, I wasn't drunk, which was a major accomplishment for me.

It was still early in LA, so I decided to tighten a few screws. In the lobby I requested a long-distance call be made to Scott Cherries's office.

"Sunny! I thought you'd be busy with all those orgies," Scott exclaimed by way of a greeting.

His voice was so distant it sounded like he was on the other side of the world, or maybe the other side of the galaxy.

"So far I haven't been able to attend any. They start after midnight, and you know I go to bed at eight o'clock, right after drinking my hot cocoa."

"And the women? There's gotta be some broad after you," Scott said.

"Just a drug addict. The rest are too busy trying to conquer the other lush, Richard Burton."

"You're not calling to wish me a happy Thanksgiving…"

"No, I already sent you a card with a turkey on it. Here they call it *guajolote*, by the way. They eat it with mole sauce, so no one can ID it during the autopsy," I joked and then swallowed hard. I don't like asking for favors. "I need to call in some of those favors you owe me," I said, seriously.

"No problem. But don't expect a tip."

"Are you still friends with that general who wanted to sell you his Korea memoirs? If so, ask him about a man—"

"If the man doesn't have a name, we can start with the phone book. Today I'll ask him for letters *a* through *f*," Scott cut in.

"Billy Joe Rogue. Claims he was a GI," I said.

"Got it."

"And how's it going with that secretary at the LA consulate?"

"If my personal life interests you, you must be really bored," Scott replied.

"Why don't you invite her out to dinner to the Luau on Rodeo Drive? I'm buying. Maybe you can while away the evening by asking her about the movie. Bring the conversation around to Stark."

"I think that'll be an interesting chat. Anything else I can do for you?"

"Tuck yourself in at night and say your prayers," I said.

He hung up the phone.

As for me, I was going to forget about that morning's unpleasantness by doing something I hadn't done since arriving in Puerto Vallarta. No, not sex; I'd given up on that already. I was going to surf.

I grabbed my good board—the other one was already kindling—put on my worn swim trunks, and strolled over to Playa de los Muertos, where some tourists, and the journalists who felt cheated by the cancellation of that day's shoot, were sunning themselves—their bodies white as sour milk.

Some local beauties played around on the seawall, their feet splashing in the water, spicing up the afternoon.

I sighed heavily and let the sound of crashing waves fill my heart before throwing myself into the water.

I mounted a tunnel and couldn't get out, the waves smacking me around. I emerged from the water and then started to turn my board to face the oncoming swell, ready to enjoy some payback. Out of the corner of my eye, I saw someone signaling me from the beach. I turned my board back around and started paddling to shore.

A smattering of applause greeted me as I walked out of the surf.

"Taking a beating from the ocean seems to me as brainless as taking a beating for sticking your nose someplace it doesn't belong," Sergeant Quintero said, beer in hand.

"Would you like to give it a try, *sargento*? It's good practice. Then when you get hit by a cop, it hurts much less."

"*Mis huevos.*"

He was already in a countdown, waiting for another opportunity to use his catchphrase.

"Isn't there any crime in this town? Shouldn't you be out looking for bad guys?"

"To be honest, it's pretty quiet. Until busybodies come and stir up the broth; that's when the scum floats to the surface." He finished his beer in one long swallow. "I came to let you know that the dead guy must have been some kind of swell."

"You mean he had a pedigree?"

"Like designer clothes, but that's not why I'm here. He was shot by a hundred-percent sterling. You won't find silver that pure in the jewelry stores here in town. I'm thinking about melting it down and having a ring made."

"A silver bullet?" I said, toweling myself off.

"I asked around at the hotels to see if they've got the Lone Ranger registered, but so far no luck. Might he be an amigo of yours?"

I was at a loss for words. I guessed Quintero didn't know the main actors in the film had all received gold revolvers loaded with silver bullets.

Running my mouth off would give him the advantage, and I didn't want that.

"Why don't you take a trip to the silver mines at Taxco? Maybe you'll get lucky and find the guilty party."

"And why don't you go straight to hell?" he said, returning the volley. No mercy. He threw his beer bottle into the sea and walked off.

I sat down on the beach and watched a pelican splash around looking for fish. A waiter from a nearby restaurant brought me a beer prepared with Tabasco sauce, lime juice, and salt.

The sunset was beautiful. As far as I was concerned, Quintero and his suspects could flush themselves down the toilet.

The sun was about to dunk itself into the sea when once again I was interrupted by my messenger boy. Picture-perfect, he still wore his old school uniform. Today his serious expression was enhanced by a finger up his nose.

"*Tengo* a message for you," he said, finding his prey and smearing it on his pants leg.

"As dependable as the telegraph. Not to mention better dressed."

"*Ellos me dijeron* they'll be waiting for you at Mismaloya, a *las diez*."

I had no idea what he was talking about. I took the brat by the shoulders and shook him a little. I didn't want to hurt him, just shake the snot loose from his pants.

"Who sent you?"

"*No sé*. They gave me this for you."

He took a wrinkled, grease-stained paper bag out of his pocket. It was fairly heavy. I stuck my hand in and felt cold steel. It was my Colt.

The kid grinned at me, sticking his hand out.

I handed him ten pesos.

By the time I'd turned back to the sea, night had fallen.

XX

KAMIKAZE

1 PART VODKA

1 PART TRIPLE SEC OR COINTREAU

1 PART LIME JUICE

Mix all the ingredients together and shake with ice. Serve in a short tequila glass. Sugar can be added for sweetening. If you prefer a fluorescent tone, add one part blue curaçao. And if you want something with more pizzazz, add "Summertime Blues" by Eddie Cochran to the mix.

The kamikaze cocktail was named after the infamous Japanese suicide pilots of World War II, since anyone who tries it gets bombed. To enhance the effect, down it in a single blow.

After a shower at the hotel, I dressed, and loaded my gun. I was ready for my date.

It was late at night when I went in search of transportation to Mismaloya. There wasn't much action at the dock. No boats were running to my destination at this time of night. I asked around, trying to find someone, among the few drunken sailors I encountered, who'd rent me a boat in exchange for a few bucks. No luck.

I was about to give up when I felt a tug on my shirt. I recognized the face at once. It was one of the kids from the Indian family I was always catching sight of near the set.

"*Señor, mi papá* says you can come with us."

The raft he pointed to was equipped with a battered outboard motor, and I could see his father trying to get it started as we spoke. The pregnant woman, with the baby in her arms, was already on board. The other two children were helping them shove off.

"*Va para Mismaloya?*" the man asked me gravely.

"I'll be able to make it worth your while if you'll take me," I said.

The man didn't answer; he simply gestured for me to climb aboard. I took my seat across from the woman, greeting her shyly. She was nursing the baby, her full, chocolate-colored breast exposed. The rest of the children were laughing in the prow. The raft was heavily laden with beans and corn, though there was no meat aboard; I imagined it didn't show up on their menu too often.

The boat sputtered and then lurched forward, moving away from the dock. The lights grew smaller and smaller, as did the noise of the city. The sea current was in our favor, and we moved at a good clip. Only a few huts on the coast were witness to our voyage to the island. It was hot and humid, but the children's laughter broke the stillness of the night.

"Do you live in Mismaloya? *Vive ahí?*" I asked, making small talk.

"*Sí, señor, mi familia* has always lived there," the man answered me dryly. The whites of his eyes shone in the darkness.

"Do you come to Vallarta often?"

"*El pulpo.* With octopus. I make a few centavos selling it to the bungalows. Before, I harvested corn, but they took the land away."

"Didn't you find work with the film shoot? Maybe they'd pay you more than what you get for selling *pulpos.*"

"I don't want nothing to do with them."

His comment was so filled with anger I decided it wise to end the conversation there.

In silence, I kept watch while the boat slowly made its way. The sound of a melancholy song grew louder, soon blanketing all of us in the boat. It was shrill and sad. A shiver ran through me, all the way from the soles of my feet to the hair on my head. I'd never quite experienced anything like it.

I turned to look at the man, and he signaled for all if us to be quiet. Then he cut the motor.

Another noise filled the air. A continuous purring that ended with a whistle. From the depths of the water, a giant shadow emerged and elevated several feet, then showed itself in all its glory. Breathless, I got to my feet. If I'd reached out, I could have touched the enormous body of the breaching whale.

It was huge. The biggest living creature I'd ever seen. I almost fell overboard when the cetacean dove back into the water, splashing us and rocking the boat. The moaning and singing continued. An enormous back emerged a few yards away, releasing a massive spray of water.

It was a herd of humpback whales, Puerto Vallarta's most famous tourists. Every year they migrate from the north in search of warm ocean currents, rather than cheap tequila and news of Burton and Taylor's sinful affair.

My heart felt like it would leap out of my chest. I turned to look at the man; he was smiling a complicit smile. The children were still pointing at the retreating whales, while we continued our trajectory toward Mismaloya.

They dropped me off at the dock by the movie set. I offered the man a five-dollar bill, but he wouldn't accept it until I agreed to take a basket of octopuses. Thankfully, they were dead.

The set was peaceful. There were only a few lights on in the technicians' houses, but the main set, the hotel where the story took place, was dark. Part of the wardrobe was hanging alongside some abandoned lights. I walked slowly, trying to make as much noise as a mouse at a veterinarian's office.

"Tell your bosses there's gonna be more accidents if we can't reach an agreement."

The voice sounded like a radio announcer's and came from a shed submerged in shadow. The accent was pure Mexico City. It was a greasy, spicy voice, like the tacos at the Plaza Mexico bullfights.

"Tell me what you want, and I'll be glad to pass it along. I'll even throw in some octopus for the grill."

"Don't get smart with me, you bum," a voice behind me growled.

I recognized it at once, a memory of an acne-riddled buttocks flashed in my mind.

"Well, if you don't want to chat, I'd better be going. Sergeant Quintero will be happy to talk to you," I bluffed without a single ace up my sleeve.

I turned around, heading back to the dock. A Luger got in my way. To my surprise, the hand that carried it was attached to a body, face and all. A razor-sharp mug, with traces of acne, and hair so greasy you could fry up an octopus on it, Spanish-style. A thin nose poked out like the barrel of a gun. An outmoded pencil mustache smiled at me above a gold tooth. He wore a shining red silk shirt, pleated pants, spats, and patent leather shoes. Antsy Underpants didn't have the kind of face you need to sell the latest fashion, but he wasn't ugly enough for his mother not to love him, either. Even rapists have mothers, I figured.

"It's bad manners to turn your back on the *licenciado*, asshole," he said, without lowering his gun.

"What else do you want? You've got the ring and the cash," I told the shadow. The Luger pressed between two of my ribs. I jumped when I felt its tickle.

"I want the roll of film, but I also want a piece of the pie. My clients are very upset. They don't like being left out," the shadow answered.

I smiled. Finally I had a pair of kings in my hand: They weren't the ones who had redecorated my hotel room. They thought the roll of film was still in my possession.

"No," I said.

The Luger dug in deeper. This time I didn't jump. I was starting to get irritated by Antsy Underpants and his routine of hassling me every time we met.

"I want the ring, the money, and another ten grand," I said boldly, feeling very macho as I laid out my bluff. The whale incident had given me courage. I heard laughter from the shadows.

Antsy didn't like me getting so high and mighty, and he dug his weapon in harder, until I could feel the barrel grazing the innermost bend of my intestines.

Then I heard blows and shouting. Two more men appeared. One looked like a judicial or federal cop: white shirt, brown pants, and a crew cut, though the shield was missing. He carried a revolver in his hand. He probably got it cheap at Woolworth's. The other guy was Gorman, looking quite a bit worse for wear.

The thug threw him at me. Gorman fell to his knees a few steps away. He was crying like a little girl whose dolly had been taken away. An ugly wound split his bald crown all the way to his forehead.

"Señor Pascal, you have no fucking idea what's at stake here...Why don't you explain it to him, Felix?" the shadow calmly declared.

I turned to look at Gorman. He hadn't gotten to his feet and was still crying. His hand was clumsily bandaged with a bloody rag. I thought he might be missing at least three fingers.

"Felix tried to be clever, too. We don't want it to end this way, right?" Antsy Underpants told me, showing his teeth.

"The ring, the money, and twenty grand."

"You said ten, or maybe your memory ain't so good?" Antsy complained.

"Plus interest for keeping me here. Another five minutes and it'll be twenty-five." I'd bluffed high. I couldn't back out now. Much less with a gun inches away from my heart. "Shoot me if you want, but you'll never get to see those photos. You know where I'm staying."

I helped Gorman to his feet. We had to get out of there. My little number was held together with safety pins as stable as a house of cards.

"Señor Pascal, you're descending into a sewer. If you're not careful, you'll get flushed out to sea," the shadow warned.

We walked away without looking back. I expected no less than a shout, a shot, or another whale popping up in front of us.

Unfortunately, it was a shot. I closed my eyes anticipating the pain.

The bullet went wide. Gorman fell to the ground. A bloody moan issued from his mouth. Another bullet passed just inches from me.

Antsy Underpants hadn't moved. He was as surprised as I was. His weapon hadn't said a word. He wasn't even aiming at me.

"There's someone else here! It's a trap, *licenciado*! Get out!" shouted the thug with the face of a judicial cop. His revolver filled the silence.

Without a second thought, I used Gorman as a shield. My Colt answered back. The bullets were all lost in the darkness of the jungle. For the third time, Antsy Underpants cleared out, leaving me behind. At least this time another guy had taken the hit.

I checked out Gorman. The bullet he took was through the forehead. Someone else had killed him.

I heard noises around me, footsteps moving off into the jungle. Others were running on the dock, and then I heard a motorboat moving away at top speed. Finally, the shouts of the technicians, roused out of bed by the gunfire, broke the night air.

I was pretty sure poor Gorman couldn't hear any of it.

XXI

PIÑA COLADA

2 OUNCES WHITE RUM

1 OUNCE COCONUT CREAM

6 OUNCES PINEAPPLE JUICE, PREFERABLY FRESH

½ CUP ICE

1 MARASCHINO CHERRY

1 PINEAPPLE SLICE

Set your blender on frappé to mix the ingredients. Serve in a tall glass, or a hollowed-out pineapple. Garnish with the maraschino cherry and pineapple slice.

The piña colada is a sweet cocktail, the perfect choice for days by the swimming pool and on the beach. It dates back to 1954, when a bartender from San Juan, Puerto Rico, tried to combine all the typical local flavors in a cocktail. He never imagined it would become such an international success. Today the piña colada is associated with nearly every tourist resort that offers picturesque beaches.

The drink was further popularized by Rupert Holmes, who released the fairly awful "Escape (The Piña Colada Song)" in 1979.

For the first time, I did the job I was paid to do; no one ended up in jail. Officially, nothing happened. No police homicide reports were filed, and the balcony accident was chalked up to just another unfortunate mishap, all too common on a film shoot.

Two days after my encounter with the whale and Antsy Underpants, the cameras were rolling. Gorman's predictions failed to come true: The supplies and food kept on coming. I even got some extra help on the job. Armed marines provided us with additional security by patrolling the vicinity in motorboats. Of course, they weren't solving any problems; they were just keeping a lid on them.

Off the record, I was asked for a thousand bucks in exchange for registering Gorman's body with the Red Cross as the victim of a traffic accident. A direct payment to Quintero. It took me a whole day to arrange. The production assistant yelled, grunted, and cursed, but finally got me in front of Stark. If Ray wanted to be in the news for the gossip, and not the murders, he'd have to pull out his wallet.

Ray Stark was not too happy to see me. The Gorman incident was bothersome enough, but when I told him there was a dead guy with one of the actors' silver bullets in him, all the color drained from his face. He coughed up the money pretty quick then, all in hundred-dollar bills.

John Huston's priority was finishing the movie; it was always finishing the movie, and he wasn't going to let a murder investigation stop him. Fortunately, in Mexico everything can be settled with dollars and a smile. You can even get a new governor that way.

Back on the film set, Stark regarded me cheerfully now that our unpleasant business was over. Richard Burton drank martinis and joked about how Liz Taylor looked like a French tart. The cinematographer Gabriel Figueroa sang excerpts from the opera *Carmen* at the top of his lungs. Deborah Kerr and Sue Lyon filmed a scene that would wind up on the cutting-room floor. And the gossip-rag photographers kept aiming their cameras at the world's most famous couple. As for me, I was stationed at the bar, finishing my martini, watching the three-ring circus I'd helped them stage.

John Huston stood next to me and said, "Keep an eye on them, Sunny. There are more reporters in Puerto Vallarta than iguanas."

I looked out over the bay. A lazy fog rolled out over the sea. A marine boat patrolled the area. Everything seemed calm, so I decided to take the first boat back to Puerto Vallarta.

When I reached my hotel, I requested a call be put through to Los Angeles. Scott Cherries didn't sound so playful this time: "What the hell is going on down there?"

"Nothing. Everything I touch turns into trouble," I replied, halfheartedly.

"I meant the film shoot. It's independent money, from New York or Chicago. The kind you need to wash and iron along with the laundry."

"The movie's funded with dirty money?"

"Stark is backed by certain groups that want to take over the studios. Sunny, the gangsters aren't like we show in the pictures anymore. No Cagney, Bogart, or Robinson. Now they're the top dogs in Hollywood."

"Thanks for the information. You can send flowers to my funeral. But no lilies; I'm allergic."

"Don't do anything rash. This isn't the first time Hollywood has used that kind of dough. It's the biggest washing machine in the world. This is basically a power struggle. If you do what's asked of you, they'll always be grateful. You'll be set for life."

"And what am I supposed to do? Die?" I asked.

"Easy, now. It's just business; some of the cash is even coming out of Mexico. My friend at the consulate told me that the Mexican government issued a land-use permit: for all of Mismaloya, a big chunk of Vallarta, and several other beaches."

"Well, I already knew they wanted to turn the set into a hotel. Stark and Huston are partners, no doubt about it. But it's bigger than all that."

"It's as big as you want it to be. In the end, it's just a movie. Do your job and don't let any of those bullets cross your path. I'll get the ice ready. You bring the tequila for the margaritas."

"Find anything out about Billy Joe Rogue?"

"I already told you the good news. He's the bad news. When I asked my friend in the military, he wanted to know who was asking. He told me if I didn't want any trouble with the government, it would be best to learn a lesson from the cat. The one curiosity killed. All he could tell me was that Rogue was in the big leagues in the Pacific. Then in Korea. Then, after the Bay of Pigs, he turned into a spook. Stay clear of him; ghosts scare me."

"I haven't felt so much at ease since I got shot with a Thompson," I said and hung up the phone. If that was good-bye, it stank. It might be the last time I'd hear my friend's voice.

I sat down at the hotel bar and introduced my face to a couple of piña coladas. They didn't do much for it, but they tasted good. Just as I finished draining my second glass, Sergeant Quintero appeared next to me. I should be more careful; I hadn't even seen him come in.

"The fatal traffic accident reports reached my desk today. I didn't like them." He ordered a beer.

"The dead guy probably liked them even less…" I laughed.

He placed a bullet in the palm of my hand. Another silver one.

"Found between the second rib and collapsed lung of your friend Felix Gorman. Something tells me a third bullet might have your name on it. No one likes a busybody."

"Neither do I, but I can't kill myself."

"This Gorman was mixed up with a gang of homosexuals, drug addicts, and gigolos in Mexico City. He was even close to Villa and Javier Nava, main suspects in the Lucerna murder. They're the kind of people we don't want here in Puerto Vallarta. This is a family town; I don't want to see it packed with perverts."

"You better start building a wall then, because a whole bunch of them already got in."

"Maybe you could lend me a hand."

"Me? Now it turns out I'm good for something after all?" I marveled.

"That ring business was a Bernabé Jurado hit. He hires those guys to steal the rocks. His faggots make nice with the ladies and clean out their jewelry boxes. I suspected that little fuck from the first murder."

"If I'm gonna be of any help at all, I'd like to know more about this Jurado guy."

"Devil's advocate. They're assholes, but he's the granddaddy of them all. He's screwed his own people. He's bailed out murderers, politicians, and perverts. The bastard weaseled his way out of jail through a loophole. He just got back from Argentina."

"And you're sure it was him?"

"Positive. He asked me to meet him tomorrow at La Palapa."

With that little gem, he'd finished his piece, looking uncomfortable, as if he were playing the fakir and had swallowed a broken sword.

"If it was a loophole, bring along a pair of handcuffs as a present and put him away for life. You might even make the papers," I suggested.

His tone of voice was flat, like he was counting boxes: "Things don't work that way down here. He already paid me what he had to pay to keep me out of it. Maybe you could do something that would get me involved, give me a hand. If he killed someone, it would help."

"Someone like me?"

"Like I said, we don't want his kind in Vallarta. Let them go on over to Acapulco. That place is already full of lowlifes." He got up, leaving a bill for his beer. "I'm just passing it along."

If he had an appointment with the devil's advocate himself, then I should bring along something heavier than my Colt. I'd need to call in some more favors, so I hopped into my Woody and went out to ask for a few.

A half an hour later, I pulled into a hellishly impoverished zone. It was all wooden huts and naked kids staring at me with big extraterrestrial eyes.

At the end of the road, on the riverbank, was a trailer home. Some forgotten furniture littered the yard, along with about a thousand empty vodka bottles.

Inside the trailer everything was surprisingly neat, though: a radio transmitter, plenty of books, and more bottles. A few photos for decoration. One showed Billy Joe shaking Kennedy's hand; another, Castro's. The one featuring Billy Joe with Marilyn Monroe impressed me the most.

"What can Billy Joe do for you, *soldado*?" the old man asked, hitching up his pants on his way out of the can.

XXII

MAI TAI

1 ½ OUNCES WHITE RUM

1 OUNCE DARK RUM

¾ OUNCE LIME JUICE

1 OUNCE GRAPEFRUIT JUICE

1 OUNCE TRIPLE SEC

1 TEASPOON FALERNUM

2 DROPS ANGOSTURA BITTERS

1 PINEAPPLE SLICE

1 MARASCHINO CHERRY

1 MINT SPRIG

Mix the first seven ingredients with ice in a blender for thirty seconds. Serve in an old-fashioned glass garnished with the pineapple slice, cherry, and sprig of mint.

The mai tai is the drink that made Oakland, California, restaurateur Trader Vic famous. Although the mai tai didn't reach its peak until 1944, Don the Beachcomber claims to have invented it in 1933. *Their recipes are different, and the flavor changes. Either way, the mai tai is yet another symbol of tiki culture. At Trader Vic's, they say that when the owner and famous mixologist Victor J. Bergeron prepared it one afternoon for some friends from Tahiti, one of them tasted it and exclaimed, "Maitai roa!" (very good!). A classic was born.*

Enjoy with another classic, Sam the Sham and the Pharaohs's "Wooly Bully."

———————————

I walked down Olas Altas Street. The buildings were as bathed in sun as their inhabitants. The heat wasn't as suffocating today, but I was drenched in sweat, nonetheless. I walked toward Pulpito Street, which rolled downhill toward the sea like a giant tongue. At the bottom stood a big palapa. My appointment was there, in that restaurant. Advertisements littered the street corners offering *pescado zarandeado* and *aguachile camarones*, typical Puerto Vallartan fare.

I ducked into the shade under the palapa roof, and cool air hit me like a snowball in the face. The restaurant was far from luxurious; even so, several swanky cars were parked outside. The entrance was on the street, but the joint also opened out onto the beach, providing a primo view of the surf. A few umbrellas were set up there, and some scantily clad bodies accompanied by cold piña coladas were catching some rays.

A girl in a crinoline skirt greeted me. She was pretty, her gray eyes contrasting with her tanned skin. Scott Cherries would have loved her.

"Welcome to La Palapa restaurant," she said amiably.

"I'm Mr. Pascal. They're expecting me."

The girl picked up a menu and guided me to a table in the middle of the restaurant. At a nearby table, a family was eating shrimp cocktail out of big round glasses, the children noisily slurping down every spoonful. At another table a lawyerly fellow, his briefcase on the table, was conversing with a local. No one there looked like a hit man.

"Can I get you something to drink?" the dark-skinned girl asked.

"Mai tai," I replied. Perhaps a little mint would freshen up this madness. The girl moved away, swishing her skirt like a rowboat lifted at high tide. The drink materialized beside me, courtesy of a tall, sullen waiter. I took a long swallow. I was still sweating.

"I've always thought that if you want to meet girls, you gotta know how to order drinks," the man with the briefcase said. His companion had vanished.

I turned around, my heart in my throat. It couldn't be a coincidence that he possessed the same voice as the man in the shadows the other night on the set.

"I like the type who can hold their liquor. You know what a woman needs to be a fun date, Sunny?"

No doubt about it, I was face-to-face with Bernabé Jurado, the devil's advocate.

"No. But I'll bet you're about to fill me in," I answered. Jurado picked up his glass and made his way over to my table, sitting down across from me.

"Booze and men." He took a long drink from his glass. All of it went down his throat, even the ice. He signaled the girl over. "Women who don't drink and don't fuck aren't worth your while."

I quickly surveyed the scene at the restaurant. It had changed a little since I'd come in. In one corner, at the restaurant entrance, was the guy who looked like a judicial police officer. He wore the same clothes. Same face. Same pistol, no doubt.

At the next table, Antsy Underpants was unfolding his napkin. Two more men had taken their positions at the beach entrance, a few yards away from us.

The girl appeared, smiling.

"Cutie, bring us a *pescado zarandeado*. Ask the chef to sear the skin golden brown. And make it a big one, 'bout seven pounds."

He turned back to me as if we were old friends. "Anything else?" he asked, adding, "I think we'll have enough on our plate with the fish; it's to die for. If you want, we can order some empanadas as an appetizer."

"I'm good," I said, as casually as I could muster.

"Bring us an order of crab empanadas while we're waiting for the fish. And since you're on your way to the kitchen, another round for me and Mr. Pascal, here. We're dehydrating in this heat."

He gave her a noisy smack on the butt, and the girl just walked away laughing. The man was charismatic, a real steamroller.

"This is the best place to eat. They make all the food for the set here."

My face gave me away.

"No, I already figured out you don't know anything," he said.

"Enlighten me. I can be a good pupil."

Bernabé Jurado laughed loudly. The family turned and stared. He winked at the kids.

"I think I haven't let them kill you just yet because you're funny, if meddlesome. In all honesty, I think I even like you, my friend."

"You don't have any friends, just potential clients."

"I like that; you oughta be a writer. I know a few. I got one out of the joint. He drank like a fish, just like you. But different, 'cause he'd try anything. From heroin to young men at the jai alai courts."

He grabbed my shoulder, as if we were drinking buddies. I felt nauseated, but I had to admit his voice was hypnotic.

"So the guy got hammered. Then it occurs to him to play William Tell with his wife. I guess you know that firing a revolver with three bottles in you is pretty much impossible. He left a hole the size of Yucatán in the woman. And guess what…"

The girl set the empanadas and drinks down on the table. Jurado smiled at her and continued his story: "That fucker Burroughs is free now. I got him out. Now he's publishing with the gringos. He sent me a copy of his goddamned book the other day. Junkie-man, or something like that. For an asshole, he isn't half-bad. You should read him." Jurado turned toward me, his voice dropping an octave. "I don't want to ruin your meal, but you do have the roll of film, don't you?"

"I'm curious about the contents," I replied. "It must be something pretty big, to kill two men over."

"Kiddo, before I took an extended vacation to Argentina, I had a nice little racket going. A girl passes for an aristocrat. She falls in with a little rich kid from the capital. We set up a show about her getting pregnant, and he pays to shut her up. Now, that was big. This is just a favor for a friend."

"And the stiffs?"

"That's another story. What we're talking about here is a lot of cash." He downed his entire glass again in one swallow. He was better than I was. Better than Richard Burton even.

"Can you imagine if they'd sold you a piece of beachfront property in Acapulco before it was what it is today? That's clean money!"

He stopped talking and devoured one of the empanadas, which were swimming in salsa, in three bites. He ordered another drink and turned to me. For him, this was just another business meeting.

"This goddamned place is a gold mine. That's why they gave them the land permit to film the movie. All the little gringos are gonna want to come to Taylor and Burton's love nest. The property is gonna cost more than the French Riviera. It's the biggest tourist project of this administration."

"And the soldiers invading the set?"

"The government wants to make sure the Mexican suppliers aren't gonna fuck it up. They'll never pay them what they owe for the film. The real investment is in the land. A whole lotta dough."

"And you are…?"

"What, aren't you working for Stark?" he asked, intrigued. "I represent the ones who want in on it: governors, senators, people from the political party. We wanna scare them a little so they'll give us a piece of the pie."

He ate another empanada. I took another look at Jurado's thugs.

They were retired cops or, worse yet, active ones. I'd turn into a juicy pork chop among crocodiles once they found out I was bluffing about that roll of film. Not much could be done; I was officially the jackass of this picture.

"Stark told me there aren't gonna be any handouts. That it's a problem for the locals to handle. He's going back to Los Angeles," I said calmly.

It sounded believable enough. Not too different from what he'd actually say.

"We'll see about that. *The Night of the Iguana* will leave Vallarta. We're staying. Either the worst SOB or the prettiest one is gonna come out on top."

He smiled. His face belonged to someone who didn't give a shit about anything, who knew he was always going to come out on top. Whereas I'd lose the game no matter what the score.

"Now hand over that roll of film so we can eat in peace," he said, tucking his napkin into the collar of his shirt.

"I want the ring and the money," I ventured.

Jurado leaned over, exasperated. "What a jackass! That Marquise of Bourbon topaz deal was my doing. There you have it. For that foul-up, I had to go on the lam to Argentina. You think I'm dumb enough to steal a goddamned ring while I'm out on parole, when what I want is millions of dollars' worth of land?"

The grim waiter arrived with a silvery tray. An enormous, gutted fish, fragrant steam rising off the dish, was in his hands. Antsy Underpants smiled at me. I already had my countdown. This would be my last supper.

Just then a new dinner guest entered from the beach. He was wearing a Santa Claus beard. Goddamned Santa. That was the signal. I jumped to my feet, grabbing the tray away from the waiter. The *zarandeado* hit Antsy Underpants smack in the face. His gun fell to the floor.

The two guys from the beach took out a shotgun and a rifle with a repeating mechanism. This was going to get noisy and ugly. Very ugly.

The judicial cop at the front door ran toward me, aiming his revolver. The shooting began. One bullet destroyed his jaw, throwing him backward. His face would never be the same. Not that I thought it mattered.

My instincts told me this wasn't the best time to knock on St. Peter's gate, so I threw myself down to the floor.

I upended the table to use it as a shield, blocking my view of my attackers as well. I prayed they weren't behind me. The shotgun fired, and the table exploded into kindling. Some of the splinters found my face. My Colt was out of my pocket; it wasn't going to catch cold today. I peeked around the table and saw the barrel of the shotgun aiming straight at me, the two black holes like the eyes of a rat. But before those eyes could do their damage, a bullet perforated another eye—the one belonging to the man holding the rifle. Blood mixed with the fish sauce.

The children's screams distracted the other guy. He didn't realize that my Colt can be fairly precise sometimes: two bullets to the chest. There were three on the ground now. Antsy Underpants must still be somewhere.

I ventured another peek. The screaming continued. People were running down the beach. Jurado was getting to his feet and swearing. There was food all over him. His impeccable suit was ruined; it hadn't been a good business meeting.

I jumped to my feet. Right across from me I spotted the familiar acne-scarred face. Shooting him at close range was a pleasure. His skull, with pieces of fish still on it, exploded like a popped balloon at the fair. I just won the grand prize.

Calm descended slowly on the restaurant. I could breathe again. I looked toward the beach. Billy Joe was putting away his old marine rifle. He took his leave once the sirens could be heard. Quintero was late, as usual.

I turned to Bernabé Jurado and held out my hand to help him to his feet. He was still trying to clean the rest of his meal off himself.

"Are you nuts, you goddamned gringo?" he yelled at me, more upset about the food stains than the shooting.

"I'm Mexican," I answered. "It'd be best if you took the beach route, seeing as how you're on parole."

For a moment he glared at me. Just for a moment. Then he picked up his briefcase, took out a card, and slid it into one of the pockets of my guayabera.

"If you ever need a lawyer, call me. I don't have any enemies either, just potential clients."

Attorney-at-law Bernabé Jurado descended the stairs to the beach. By the time the cops arrived, he was out of sight. He'd stuck me with the bill.

XXIII

SANGRITA, TEXAS-STYLE

TEQUILA

2 CUPS FRESH ORANGE JUICE

3 TABLESPOONS GRENADINE

¼ TABLESPOON HOT SAUCE

1 CUP TOMATO JUICE

3 TABLESPOONS SALT

1 LIME SLICE

*B*lend all the ingredients except for the tequila. Serve along-side the tequila in a separate glass with ice. Garnish with the slice of lime.

This recipe is a variation on the original sangrita and can be found at any bar in Texas or along the US-Mexico border. Its distinguishing ingredient is the addition of grenadine. Like the original, Jalisco version, this concoction has a strong, spicy flavor. While this combination would be sacrilege in Jalisco, folks along the border regions swear by it. It tastes even better accompanied by Elvis Presley's "Mexico."

I pulled up outside Kimberly House, the great mango tree still preying on unwary pedestrians. I stopped a moment just outside its wide canopy. I could tell it was laughing at me, just waiting for me to cross beneath. I didn't fall for it, though, opting to walk around it instead.

I rang the bell by the door, and the tree sighed in frustration, a wormy mango dropping a few feet away from me.

I waited a few minutes, and then finally heard steps coming toward the door. It was thrown wide open, and I found myself standing before my favorite gorilla, Bobby La Salle. When he saw me, he smiled his boyish gap-toothed grin.

"Mr. Burton and Miss Taylor are down on the beach," he said reflexively, before even greeting me. I pounded him on the back affectionately and entered the house through the noodle-sized gap left between him and the door frame.

"Good morning, Bobby. I'll wait inside," I said in Spanish. He didn't stop me, just stood there trying to make out my words, as if I'd spoken to him in ancient Aramaic. I took long strides toward the patio, and Bobby trotted after me, apparently giving up on the translation. I went straight to the bar, found the bottle of raicilla, and poured two shot glasses' worth.

"I think it would be better if you came back later," he suggested.

"I don't have much to do," I replied. "Yesterday I shot the guts out of three men. Killing makes me thirsty."

I slid his drink over to him. Mine had already disappeared down my throat. "Won't you join me?"

Bobby Gorilla stared at the glass as if I were tempting him with the forbidden apple. His hands twitched nervously, his fingers intertwining like a ball of snakes.

"Maybe Mr. Burton wouldn't mind."

"That's the spirit, compadre," I said, again in Spanish, while pouring another. He choked it down like bitter medicine. I took a seat on one of the chintzy leather-and-wood chairs on the terrace, crossed my legs, and sighed. The day was hot, but a fresh breeze drove away the impulse to throw myself headfirst into the sea. Bobby didn't sit down.

"I came to have a chat with Mr. Burton, myself, because the cops would like to ask him a few questions." I tossed it out as if we were talking about the weather.

"What kind of questions?"

"The dead guy they found in the river was part of a gang of jewel thieves from Mexico City. The secret of Miss Taylor's ring floated away down the river, next to that stiff."

"Yeah, I bet that ring is long gone," the gorilla grunted.

I stood up to serve myself another raicilla and thought how glorious it would be with a decent sangrita.

"Then again, the possibility occurs to me that the ring in question didn't go far, I said, turning my back to him. "Maybe it just took a few steps, and it's still here in this house."

The raicilla spilled over the edge of the glass, leaving a white mark on the wooden bar. There was no noise behind me. Not even the sound of his breathing. All that silence made me uncomfortable. I spun around. He was inches away, holding his breath.

I downed my drink.

Bobby started breathing again.

"Yesterday a certain lawyer told me that no one turned the ring over to him. So then I thought, does Bobby really think they're gonna be able to fence it back in LA, like some trinket?" I gave it straight to him, figuring that even if he did have a baby face that was no reason to treat him like one. "That little item is worth a sum you'll never see, not in your entire life, not even if you won the heavyweight championship three times over."

His fists crunched closed. He wasn't angry, though. His expression was one of fear and amazement. Heavy on the fear.

"I don't know what you're talking about."

"Is it a woman?" I asked. "Do you have gambling debts? I'm sure your boss would lend the money to you. I can tell he's fond of you. You're his three-hundred-and-fifty-pound mascot. You bring him the newspaper, you serve the margaritas, and you go deliver the ransom money for a piece of jewelry."

The fear started to show in his eyes. Two veins the size of a highway jumped out of the back of his neck. His arm started swinging like a jackhammer. He was turning into a locomotive without brakes, about to run me over.

I hoped for a miracle.

That miracle had a pair of violet eyes. Liz Taylor appeared on the scene, dressed in a long red camisole and flanked by three children so caked in sand they looked like sugar doughnuts. She roared into the house like a thunderstorm, barking orders to her children, who leaped around like forlorn little lambs. Richard Burton brought up the rear with the rest of the entourage, a bevy of assistants all carrying baskets, hats, and umbrellas.

Burton saw me. Wearing a big grin, he came over to where we stood. Bobby relaxed, but he didn't take his eyes off me.

"You in a hurry? You couldn't wait for me to get back to start knocking them back." He turned to his bodyguard. "Bobby, get me two glasses of raicilla."

Bobby didn't move. Nothing, not a blink. His eyes were still glued to me.

The actor paused, then impatiently moved to pour the drinks himself.

"I'm here because I've got some good news," I told him, raising my glass.

His mouth opened up like a well, and the liquor vanished inside. He slammed the shot glass down on the table, releasing a huge guffaw. He gave me a big bear hug that lifted me up off the ground.

"I knew I could trust you, son. Your kind never fails me. Did you find it?"

He set me back down on the ground and took a seat in one of the chairs. His entourage positioned themselves all around. One of them was Taylor's ex-husband and the father of two of her children. Taylor continued ordering the children around. Bobby remained stock-still.

"I found it. Not without the help of Bobby La Salle," I exclaimed. "That's why I wanted to get here early, so I could thank him in person. Did you hear about the shoot-out?"

"Who hasn't? You're already a legend in Puerto Vallarta."

"That's where they caught the thieves. Bobby's description was what led to their arrest."

Burton turned to his favorite bodyguard. He looked like the proud father of the guy who just made the winning goal. Bobby couldn't so much as swallow.

"I'd like to ask you a favor, Mr. Burton. I heard about John Huston's gift, the gold pistols. I'd like to see yours. I'm a big fan of collectible weapons."

Burton turned to his bodyguard. "Show it to him, Bobby."

La Salle hesitated, moving one foot only slightly, as if struggling with himself, then he disappeared into another room, glaring at me as he left.

"I gave it to Bobby for safekeeping. There are children in the house. We don't want any accidents."

Bobby returned with a fine wood case. He opened it and reluctantly handed it to me. Inside, on a bed of felt, rested a gold-plated .22 pistol. It wasn't as shiny as I'd hoped, but I couldn't deny it was interesting. And inside the cylinder were bullets as silver as Taxco's finest. One was missing. In its place was the shiniest piece of all, a ring with pearls and gems as big as a cluster of grapes. The kind of ring only Elizabeth Taylor would have. In one smooth movement, I set the box down on the bar and took up the pistol. It had a spicy smell…

"Beautiful piece."

"It's a twenty-two, only good for killing birds and frightening away thieves," Burton said disdainfully.

"Don't you believe it; from a few feet away, it can put a hole in your gut." I turned to look at Bobby. The fear in his eyes had turned to admiration. He started trembling when I playfully pointed the gun at him.

"That madman Huston thinks it's a funny joke," Burton declared. "But to me it was the most idiotic thing he could have done. I'm keeping it as a consolation prize if they don't give me an award for this film."

I returned the gun to its case and closed it. I took one step toward Burton, holding out my hand. The ring was in my palm. He didn't take it. His assistant picked it up with a handkerchief, as if it might be infected.

"I gotta go now," I said.

"Good work, son," Burton said, ignoring my outstretched hand. I was no longer a friend, just another member of the film crew. The same old story. I didn't mind. I just headed for the door. I could feel Bobby breathing down my neck. I opened the front door. Outside, the mango tree was already waiting for me. From the threshold, Bobby called, "What happens now?"

"You go back to your boss; play a game of Ping-Pong. You're going to have to come up with a good excuse to explain why one of those silver bullets is missing, other than leaving it in the body of some two-bit crook you hired to set up the whole ransom scenario."

Bobby kept watching me from the other side of the door. "It wasn't my idea. They asked me to do it."

"I know, but it was your idea to keep the ring." I wasn't letting him off that easy. "You didn't count on him bringing someone else along, someone who'd take us both on in order to keep the dough for himself. Bad luck; next time you'd better ask your partners in crime for references."

I took several steps toward my Woody. Bobby ran after. He put one hand on my shoulder, stopping me in my tracks. He turned me around, took an envelope out of his pocket, and placed it in my hand. It was the cash.

"I killed him in self-defense. They didn't take the money from me. I hid it in the car before we got to the drop-off. Keep it. I owe you one."

I smiled. The gorilla wasn't so dumb after all. With a few more classes, he might even learn to juggle and do tricks. I handed back the money.

"Pay that debt. If there's any cash left over, drop by my studio in Venice Beach. You can buy me a couple of rounds at Trader Vic's."

I climbed into my Woody. A rotten mango dropped onto the hood.

XXIV

SALTY DOG

1 PART GIN OR VODKA

3 PARTS GRAPEFRUIT JUICE

SALT

Mix the gin with the juice in a tall glass with ice and salt around the rim.

A variation on the classic greyhound, the salty dog is a wartime creation, conceived in the Pacific theater, where grapefruit juice was abundant. In the 1950s, it made its debut at various golf tournaments in Palm Springs, offering a refreshing respite after long, eighteen-hole walks in the hot desert sun. Enjoy in the company of Dean Martin and his hit "Everybody Loves Somebody."

The case was closed. Elizabeth Taylor's renowned ring was back with its owner. The gang of lowlifes who made a buck by selling drugs, blackmailing people, and stealing their jewels was either broken up or its members killed off as scores were settled. They had been the ones running "the Infamous House of Vice" and recruiting girls as prostitutes. Quintero even dared to name Mr. Antsy Underpants as none other than the man responsible for the Lucerna Street murder, a notoriously unsolved slaying in Mexico City. No one believed him.

Though everyone liked the story. Except me. But who was I to talk? I had other fish to fry.

I crossed the set without looking at anyone, not even Ava Gardner, who was once again resting her seductive butt on the hammock by Sue Lyon's bungalow. Another hit was on the record player, but this time it was "Devil in Disguise." Elvis Presley singing about a diabolical woman. He was always right.

Several flower arrangements decorated the joint, including some stunning lilies. The loveliest flowers always smell like death. Blondie was on a deck chair reading a novel in French. I didn't understand the title, but I recognized the author: Anaïs Nin.

"Doggie, you've finally come to visit me," she said, opening her olive-colored eyes.

She was wearing a striped sailor blouse and white shorts, short enough to make a man sweat. She'd pulled back her golden hair with a ribbon that matched the smile clenched around her cigarette, waiting for me to light it. But Blondie was a tough cookie; she wouldn't wait for long.

A glass with two enormous ice cubes rested beside her. I raised it and took a sip: a salty dog. I wouldn't have expected any less from her.

"I didn't want to disturb you. In the end, it worked out okay. Just another bluff by a gang of lousy card players. One thing's for sure: they should never have tried to play poker with John Huston," I said by way of a greeting.

"What? Huston? What's he got to do with all this?"

I ignored her question.

"I guess I oughta thank you for not telling on me. The cops don't like me; they can't stand a free spirit," she said with a touch of intellectual aloofness. Which didn't bother me. On the contrary, her malice was what turned me on.

"I know. But you can keep the thanks; I was just doing my job."

"I'll have to find some other way to repay you then. Any ideas?" she asked, whispering.

I moved closer and picked her up. I gave her a long kiss.

"The women I want and the ones I get live in different worlds," I murmured into her ear. She trembled. She was still holding her cigarette between her fingers.

She said, "Why are you afraid of me?"

"Because you're the kind who kills. And I know you did." I gave her a cold smile.

"That…I don't know what you're talking about," she said in a low voice, her expression turned feline, like a tiger ready to pounce.

"To you, we're stepping-stones in life. Throwaways you no longer have any use for, like poor Gorman. He just wanted to make a few bucks peddling dope to the film crew. It never occurred to him you wanted more. That's why he took you to that house."

Blondie narrowed her eyes.

"You must have owed them plenty to have to pay them that way. Sex for drugs is like bribery. But bribery doesn't have such a foul stench."

"You'll never get it. This is Hollywood. You need something harder than booze to be able to stand it."

"Tell that to Gorman," I spat. "Sure, it would have been easier if you hadn't shot him."

Her face had turned into a piece of bitter fruit. Poisoned.

"You see, they thought he had the roll of film. It must have hurt quite a bit while they were asking him about it. Don't bother explaining. I don't really care if you killed him because he knew too much, because of your debts, or because you felt like it. You used Sue Lyon's golden pistol. I realized that you two had a lot in common, your Zippo, the drugs, and the gun."

"What do you want to keep your big mouth shut?" she said, serious now, moving away from me as if I were a leper.

"You were the one who sent the boy to tell me to come to the set, where Jurado and his thugs were waiting to drop me. I wanted you to know that I'm not just another guy you can throw away. I didn't buy your little song and dance. I want the roll of film. That'll do."

She took the golden pistol out of the desk and smiled at me.

"I saved you. Fancher was with me. The second shot was for you. He wanted to impress his girlfriend."

"I'll be grateful the rest of my life, doll." I took two steps toward her. The pistol was still aimed at me. So were the olive eyes.

"Take it easy. They're not going to put you in a Mexican jail. Hand over the roll; the rest doesn't matter anymore."

"What makes you think I have it?"

I told her that only Antsy Underpants, she, and I were in that house. "The girl doesn't count. You were the only one who could have gotten into my room to look for it." I took another step. The pistol touched my stomach.

"You're still a loser. You always will be." Her voice was no more than a sigh. Without lowering the weapon, she took the roll out of the desk and handed it over. Our faces were just inches apart. She lowered the gun. For a moment, I felt a great urge to kiss her again, but I turned instead and left the bungalow.

She could have shot me in the back right then. I guess there must have been something between us after all, because she didn't squeeze the trigger.

I crossed the terrace in a rage. I wanted to get as far away as possible from the place; I'd go straight to Puerto Vallarta to drain the bar at my hotel. I felt dirty, covered in the kind of dirt you can't wash away.

But John Huston stopped me cold. Stark was right behind him with a flock of assistants. It wasn't a good time to get in my way.

"Pascal, I need you to go pick up Tennessee Williams at the airport. He's pitching a fit because I gave his story a happy ending."

"I'm not in the mood today," I said without thinking and pushing past him.

"Excuse me? Stop fooling around and do as I say, wino."

Without missing a beat, I doubled back to face the director. I had to elevate my fist to connect a punch to his jaw. The bastard was as tall as a goddamned palm tree.

To my surprise, I almost managed to knock him down; I knew he was an expert boxer. But when you're really pissed off, you can get pretty rough.

"This is all bullshit. You planned the ring heist to throw me off the scent. Even the goddamned ransom money came from the production. Not too many hundred-dollar bills circulating in this town, right?" I grunted, gritting my teeth.

Stark simply closed his eyes.

"The movie stuff is a smoke screen so guys like you can get rich off of other people's land. Hollywood isn't making a goddamned movie in Puerto Vallarta; it's making its very own Puerto Vallarta."

"Pascal, you're fired," Huston told me, with all the majesty of a god crushing a mere mortal. Stark remained silent; to him, I was insignificant as well. Not even worth a retake.

"Maybe you're right. At least the movie gets to have a happy ending." I couldn't resist one last parting shot: "Besides, Mr. Huston, you're a poor poker player. I was on to you by the time the second hand was dealt."

The pained look on his face was reward enough. *Más o menos*. I got the hell out of Mismaloya.

XXV

GIBSON

6 PARTS VODKA

1 PART VERMOUTH

2 PICKLED ONIONS

Mix the vodka and vermouth with ice in a cocktail shaker, blending until chilled. Serve in a cocktail glass. Garnish with the onions on a toothpick and the single "What Am I Supposed to Do" by Ann-Margret.

The Gibson was baptized in the speakeasies in Chicago during Prohibition. The name comes from the drink's small onions, thought to resemble the breasts of the ubiquitous Gibson Girl. During the two first decades of the twentieth century, the Gibson Girl was rendered by the famous Life *magazine illustrator Charles Dana Gibson, thus her moniker. The personification of feminine beauty at the time, many models posed for Gibson, including Anaïs Nin. Another illustrator, Harry G. Peter, used the Gibson Girl as his inspiration for the Wonder Woman comics.*

Back at the hotel, I got a cold and lonely reception. Maybe I needed a pet, something to keep me company. That's what I was thinking about as I started to pack my belongings.

I decided I wasn't going to let those bastards off that easy, though. Before leaving, I'd have my vengeance on them. I'd leave them such a huge bill they'd be able to film another *Night of the Iguana* with it.

Down at the bar, I ordered a Gibson, a salty dog, and a gimlet. The drinks didn't last longer than a heartbeat. I downed all three. And that was just the beginning.

"If you really must drink all the alcohol in the world, you could have invited me along. I can be helpful when I want to be," said the voice, the one best heard from up close. I raised my eyes and then drowned in her deep, dark ones. Ava Gardner sat down beside me. She didn't need an invitation, for that or anything else she might want to do.

Her dark hair was bound under a patterned scarf, and she wore a loose silk blouse that revealed her faultless cleavage and a wide skirt that showed off her perfectly engineered legs.

"I figured I'd have to call your agent first and send him a list of cocktails for his approval," I answered, unsmiling.

Ava Gardner lifted her cigarette to her mouth with the delicacy of a hummingbird.

"Don't you believe it. Deep down I'm very superficial," she quipped, gracing me with her best magazine-cover smile. The smoke trailed toward my face. It tasted glorious.

The barman set down another three glasses in front of me and a manhattan in front of her. Gardner didn't drink it right away. She reached for the cherry first, biting down on it seductively with lips painted the same dark red hue as the fruit.

"I heard you're unemployed." She crossed her legs; I'm not sure whether it was meant provocatively or not, but it made me lose my train of thought.

"News flies. Are they using messenger pigeons now?" I responded sarcastically. I'm not the kind of guy who gets dinner and a date with this woman. She was with me on a whim, like a cat at the dog pound. "I don't mean to be rude. Your company is a million-dollar prize, maybe more. But you're not here to have a drink with me."

"You think I'd never notice a man like you?"

"I think we're on different levels. About forty floors apart," I replied. "In my experience, the people in the penthouse don't generally scout out the basement."

"I was a country girl once. I've still got the simple tastes of a country girl." She took a drag. "You've got something that could really get to me."

"I can think of plenty of things. If you want me to say something to make you blush, be more specific."

"The roll of film. I know you found it," she said, looking off into the distance.

"Is everyone on that roll of film?" I didn't have anything to lose. I got up and flashed her a smile. "You've been in more beds than a traveling salesman: Sinatra, Hughes, and that bullfighter whose name I can't remember. They don't need to remind you of your reputation. Why would anyone want to blackmail you? For that, you need to be squeaky clean, something you haven't been since sometime after the third martini." I felt dizzy. My head was as heavy as a cement mixer.

"You're wrong. The less you've got, the more you pay for it."

That was the last thing I heard. That final drink was a little stronger than usual.

When I woke up, I was back in my room and submerged in water. A few bubbles floated to the surface. The window across from me was dark. I raised myself up a bit, trying not to breathe, worried I'd drown. But I took in a great gulp of air anyway. The water wasn't there, and neither were the bubbles. I fell back into bed and started laughing.

A few minutes later, I mustered the strength to get up again. It hadn't been such a strong narcotic after all. The drugs were no longer interfering with my senses.

A pistol was. It was aimed directly at my face. It was my Colt, and behind it was Billy Joe, sitting on the edge of my bed. This time he wasn't wearing his Santa expression. He'd exchanged it for a tough, military face.

"Soldier, you had something that didn't belong to you," he told me, speaking exclusively in English for the first time. "It's already been destroyed."

"Which side are you on? Ducks or hunters?"

I really wasn't surprised to see him there. Apparently, it was becoming a habit with him.

"Nothing personal. We're colleagues, soldier. You were in charge of making sure nothing happened on the set. I, on the other hand, was working to make sure everything here followed the script as planned. Today, it's here in Puerto Vallarta. Yesterday, it was Paris. Tomorrow, it'll be Turkey, or someplace or another."

"Who do you work for? The mob? The US government?"

"I'm a free agent. I work for the highest bidder."

He gave me a look and handed me my pistol. My suitcase sat in a corner, just like the rest of my belongings. I was already history.

"The photos in your trailer that night I went to ask you for help. I saw them. You weren't lying to me about Kennedy. You worked for him."

"Yeah, in Cuba. Then in Berlin. Good man; he liked his martinis dry."

He got up and tucked his dog tags into his T-shirt. Then he smiled again, this time like the goddamned Santa Claus I knew so well.

"Is this the end...? I can't believe it. These people are going to destroy the place. They'll buy hotels, properties, and they'll stick you in jail. They think it's just a Monopoly game."

"This is our world. If you don't like it, you can get off whenever you want," the old man said.

"What was on that roll? Why did they want it so badly? It wasn't just Ava Gardner. Photos of some big shot?" I asked, thinking that at least I deserved an explanation.

"Don't know. Don't care. It's like when you picked up those pictures in Tijuana."

He knew about my last job. This guy knew more than the devil himself, and it wasn't just because he was such an old cuss.

He opened the door of the room and gave me one last, paternal look.

"I'm getting too old for this shit. Maybe I could use a partner... You already know where I live."

He left without closing the door.

XXVI

IGUANA MARTINI

6 OUNCES GIN

5 DROPS TABASCO SAUCE

2–3 DROPS LIME JUICE

1 PEELED SHRIMP, GRILLED

1 LIME SLICE

Mix the gin with the Tabasco sauce and lime juice in a blender with ice. Serve in a cocktail glass. Garnish with the shrimp, the slice of lime, and the sixties hit "Surfin' Bird" by The Trashmen.

This drink was born in the 1960s in Puerto Vallarta, when the beach town became one of the main tourist attractions in Mexico after John Huston filmed The Night of the Iguana *there. The romance between Richard Burton and Liz Taylor got a lot of press, providing great publicity for the resort. The creator of the iguana martini was a local restaurant owner who got his start with a small seafood grill, thus the creative addition of a grilled shrimp garnish. The inspiration for the cocktail came from one of the restaurateur's best customers, an amateur surfer who worked as head of security for the famous film.*

The sun rose behind me, illuminating the bay. I'd been waiting for daybreak on the beach just outside town so I could catch the early-morning surf. The waves were small, peaceful, as if they were playing at slower revolutions than the rest of the world.

After several hours lost in my own world, I came back to reality, collapsing contentedly on the beach and reaching for my last bottle of gin. My Woody was waiting on the access road, along with what few belongings I had. Ready to go back home, or to whatever else was out there.

Some of the rustic palapas that sold grilled seafood were starting to come to life. The smell of freshly made tortillas reeled me in to one. Inside it was hot from the grill, but I found myself surrounded by familiar faces. The family that had given me a ride on the boat that fateful night was there. When he saw me, the man smiled, and the kids ran around me, cheerfully shouting and laughing.

The woman was preparing the tortillas, taking advantage of the fact that the baby was asleep by her side.

"*Buenos días,*" I said, sitting down on an old wooden chair.

"*Buenos días, señor,*" the father replied, still smiling. Seeing him made me remember our encounter with the whale. For me, it had been a magical moment; for them, just another day living in paradise.

"And what are you doing here? *Qué estas haciendo?*"

"Here, *ya ve,*" he responded matter-of-factly, as always.

I ate beans and tacos with shrimp and octopus near the grill, the soft breeze off the ocean caressing my face. And hot coffee spiced with cinnamon worked its magic. I paid with a ten-dollar bill, refusing to accept the change.

I stretched out my arms lazily, bottle of gin in hand, and walked toward the edge of the water. Mornings in Puerto Vallarta are beautiful. The place was worth every centavo, every drop of blood. I took another swallow, a long one, and threw the bottle into the sea as far as I could. I watched the waves drag it away until it was lost from sight.

I hadn't liked that last swallow. There are times when not even all the booze in the world can take away the bitter aftertaste of life.

LAST CALL

I first read Raymond Chandler when I was twenty-five. All of his novels, in one month. The next month, I read the entire Belascoarán series by Paco Ignacio Taibo II. When I went backpacking in Europe, I carried along a copy of *The Long Goodbye* and another of *Some Clouds*. They changed my life. I was falling in love with the genre. This novel is a tribute to both writers. I'd like to think that even after all the blending their flavor can still be savored.

Most of the characters in this story existed; they did and said what's written here. Sometimes reality surpasses fiction. It's up to every reader to discover how much of this is true and how much is the product of my imagination.

Like all good cocktails, this novel features several ingredients. The main one was Bernardo Fernández's insistence that I write it. His support and years of teaching have made me less of a hack. There's also the encouragement I received from Francisco Ruiz Velazco, Bachan, and Edgar Clement.

I genetically inherited a taste for martinis from my grandfather, journalist Eduardo Correa. He wanted one of his grandchildren to be a writer. Unfortunately, I wasn't on the top of his list. I hope he takes it philosophically. Wherever he may be, I'm sure they prepare the best martinis.

I'd like to thank the Reeds for the information and anecdotes about old Vallarta, and also Scott Cherrin, for giving me a copy of *John Huston, King Rebel*. My thanks to Pepe Quintero for inspiring his character, to the entire city of Puerto Vallarta for assimilating a strange beast like me, and to Sonia Diego and Tanya Huntington because they made this a better book. And, of course, to my accomplice in life and my harshest critic: Lillian. I love her even more since she decided we should leave the Condesa neighborhood in Mexico City and go live in Vallarta, and later, in Tehuacán. Since then, my life hasn't gotten any easier, but it's a lot more fun.

Salud!

F. G. Haghenbeck
Puerto Vallarta, Mexico City, Los Angeles, 2005–6

ABOUT THE AUTHOR

Photograph © Lillyan Funes, 2009

F. G. Haghenbeck was born in Mexico City. He's been an architect, museum designer, freelance editor, and TV producer. He's also the comic book writer of *Crimson* and *Alternation*, as well as a Superman series for DC Comics. John Huston biographer William Reed encouraged Haghenbeck to transition into writing crime novels, and the result is *Bitter Drink*, which has already won the Turn of the Screw Crime Novel Award in Mexico.

Haghenbeck currently works full time writing novels and editing historical and pop-culture books. He loves eating his wife's gourmet food, drinking cocktails, reading the noir novels of Raymond Chandler and Paco Ignacio Taibo II, and watching cartoons with his daughter, Arantza.